THE ENCHANTED WORLD OF HONEY MOON™

STICKY SITUATION

by

Suzanne Brooks Kuhn

with Joyce Magnin

Illustrations by Becky Minor
Based on the artwork of Christina Weidman

Created by Mark Andrew Poe

rabbit publishers

Sticky Situation (The Enchanted World of Honey Moon)
by Suzanne Brooks Kuhn
Created by Mark Andrew Poe

Rabbit Publishers
1624 W. Northwest Highway
Arlington Heights, IL 60004

Illustrations by Becky Minor
Based on the artwork of Christina Weidman
Cover and Interior Design by Lewis Design & Marketing

ISBN: 978-1-943785-20-9

10 9 8 7 6 5 4 3 2 1

1. Fiction - Action and Adventure 2. Children's Fiction
First Edition
Printed in U.S.A.

"Don't worry, Honey Moon.
I got you covered."
— *Turtle*

TABLE OF CONTENTS

PREFACE

Halloween visited the little town of Sleepy Hollow and never left. Many moons ago, a sly and evil mayor found the powers of darkness helpful in building Sleepy Hollow into "Spooky Town," one of the country's most celebrated attractions. Now, years later, the indomitable Honey Moon understands she must live in the town but she doesn't have to like it, and she is doing everything she can to make sure that goodness and light are more important than evil and darkness.

Welcome to *The Enchanted World of Honey Moon*. Halloween may have found a home in Sleepy Hollow, but Honey and her friends are going to make sure it doesn't catch them in its Spooky Town web.

FAMILY

Honey Moon

Honey is ten years old. She is in the fifth grade at Sleepy Hollow Elementary School. She loves to read, and she loves to spend time with her friends. Honey is sassy and spirited and doesn't have any trouble speaking her mind—even if it gets her grounded once in a while. Honey has a strong sensor when it comes to knowing right from wrong and good from evil and, like she says, when it comes to doing the right thing—Honey goes where she is needed.

Harry Moon

Harry is Honey's older brother. He is thirteen years old and in the eighth grade at Sleepy Hollow Middle School. Harry is a magician. And not just a kid magician who does kid tricks, nope, Harry has the true gift of magic.

Harvest Moon

Harvest is the baby of the Moon family. He is two years old. Sometimes Honey has to watch him but she mostly doesn't mind.

II

Mary Moon

Mary Moon is the mom. She is fair and straightforward with her kids. She loves them dearly, and they know it. Mary works full-time as a nurse, so she often relies on her family for help around the house.

John Moon

John is the dad. He's a bit of a nerd. He works as an IT professional, and sometimes he thinks he would love it if his children followed in his footsteps. But he respects that Harry, Honey, and possibly Harvest will need to go their own way. John owns a classic sports car he calls Emma.

Half Moon

Half Moon is the family dog. He is big and clumsy and has floppy ears. Half is pretty much your basic dog.

FRIENDS

Becky Young

Becky is Honey's best friend. They've known each other since pre-school. Becky is quiet and smart. She is an artist. She is loyal to Honey and usually lets Honey take the lead, but occasionally Becky makes her thoughts known. And she has really great ideas.

Claire Sinclair

IV

Claire is also Honey's friend. She's a bit bossy, like Honey, so they sometimes clash. Claire is an athlete. She enjoys all sports but especially soccer, softball, and basketball. Sometimes kids poke fun at her rhyming name. But she doesn't mind—not one bit.

Brianna Royal

Brianna is also one of Honey's classmates. Brianna is different from all the other kids. She definitely dances to her own music. Brianna is very special. She seems to know things before they happen and always shows up in the nick of time when a friend is in trouble.

FOES

Clarice Maxine Kligore

Clarice is Honey's arch nemesis. For some reason Clarice doesn't like Honey and tries to bully her. But Honey has no trouble standing up to her. The reason Clarice likes to hassle Honey probably has something to do with the fact that Honey knows the truth abut the Kligores. They are evil.

Maximus Kligore

V

The Honorable (or not-so-honorable depending on your viewpoint) Maximus Kligore is the mayor of Sleepy Hollow. He is the one who plunged Sleepy Hollow into a state of eternal Halloween. He said it was just a publicity stunt to raise town revenues and increase jobs. But Honey knows different. She knows there is more to Kligore's plans—something so much more sinister.

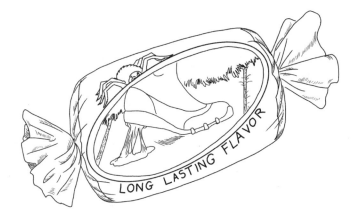

LONG LASTING FLAVOR

THE NEW GIRL

Honey stopped and scraped her shoe on a rock.

"Gum. I hate sticky gum," she said.

"Looks like Mummy Mint," Claire said.

Ugh, Honey pulled and pulled and finally the sticky, green goo released its barnacle hold on her brand new Sketcher.

"Look at the size of that wad," Claire commented. "It's like the person was chewing the entire pack."

Honey dropped the giant wad into the trash receptacle and then wiped her fingers on the grass. "It was probably that new girl. She is always chewing gum—even in class. And not a single teacher makes her spit it out."

"Yeah, it's like she's a princess or something."

Honey slung her turtle backpack over her shoulder. "Oh, she's a princess all right. The Princess of the Kingdom of Annoyance. She's like that gum. She keeps sticking to me. Won't leave me alone. Even after I told her."

Claire laughed. "Yeah, I noticed. And speaking of which, don't look now but there she is." Claire pointed across the Town Green. Sure enough the new girl, Darcy Diamond, was waving like mad.

"Geeze," Honey said. "You'd think she's

2

trying to land a 747."

"What should we do? Run?"

Honey took a breath. "Yeah. Maybe if we run we can be at my house before she catches up."

They took off. They ran hard. But just as they reached Shopper's Row, Darcy appeared from behind a tree.

3

"Where ya goin'?" Darcy asked. "I was hollering for you to wait up. But you didn't. Guess you didn't hear me. Where ya goin'? Can I come too?"

Honey gave herself a face palm. "Where did you come from?"

"Over there. I saw you run. So I ran too. Wanna play?"

"Wanna play?" Claire said. "What are you? Six?"

Darcy shook her head. "No. I'm ten. Just like you guys, unless you're already eleven. I'm still ten. What are you? My birthday is in December. When's yours?"

Honey stamped her foot. "Look, Darcy. We are going to my house, and my mom only lets me have one friend over at a time." Honey swallowed. It was a lie. She could have two friends in when Mom was at work.

4

Darcy's mouth turned into a perfect pout, complete with a quivering bottom lip. A sure fire way to get your own way. Honey figured Darcy for a professional pouter if she ever saw one. But she was not going to fall for Darcy's drama.

"Oh, so you're a drama queen?" Honey said.

Claire nudged Honey. "That's your thing, Honey."

Honey shot Claire a scathing glare.

"No, I'm not a drama queen," Darcy said. "I'm just new and...well, I just want to hang out."

"You still can't come, Darcy."

Honey swallowed. She kind of felt bad. Still, Darcy was kind of a pest, and she just wasn't in the mood for entertaining pests.

"Oh, that's okay," Darcy said looking at her feet. "I'll catch ya later."

"Great." Claire grabbed Honey's hand, and she and Honey took off like rockets toward Honey's house. They did make one quick stop at Spooky Sweets. Honey bought seven chocolate peanut butter spiders and three Sleepy Hollow Red Fish—they had teeth. Claire bought the same but added one soft, caramel brain.

"Good Old Sleepy Hollow," Honey said. "Sometimes living in a town where it's Halloween every day kinda works."

When they got to Honey's house, they stopped dead in their tracks. Harry, Honey's older brother, was on the front lawn practicing one of his magic acts. There was a small group of kids assembled around him. It wasn't easy having a magician for a brother, especially when he felt like showing off on the front lawn.

"Jumpin' tiddlywinks!" Honey said. "What is he doing?"

"Looks like he's working on some kind of vanishing act," Claire said. "Cool. Let's watch." She bit into a Sleepy Hollow Red Fish.

Honey shook her head. Talk about pests. Harry had a way of interfering with Honey's life at times. She loved her brother and would do pretty much anything for him, but most of the time, Harry was a pest.

Harry stood next to a tall, wood box that sort of resembled a coffin. He wore his velvet cape that Honey's mom had made especially for him. He pointed his magic wand at the box and said, "Abracadabra, I command you to RETURN!"

Then he spun the box around three times, tapped it with the magic wand three times,

and opened the door. Everyone applauded except Honey. She was utterly dumbfounded and could not believe her eyes. Standing inside the box, grinning like a jack-o'-lantern, was Darcy Diamond!

"What in the world?" Honey said. "How did she get there?"

"That's quite a trick," Claire said. "We just left her at the Green."

Honey stamped her foot. "I knew we shouldn't have stopped for candy."

"Awwww, who cares? She just ran really fast, that's all."

"But don't you get it? She ran to *my* house. She won't take no for an answer."

Darcy stood next to Harry. He grabbed her hand and thrust it into the air in triumph as the crowd cheered.

"Come on," Honey said. "Let's get inside before she sees us."

But it was too late.

"Honey, Honey," Darcy called. "Wait up."

"Quick," Claire said. "Let's make a run for the backyard."

Darcy bolted after them. "Wait, wait. I want to play."

Honey stood at the back door as Darcy caught up. "Now look, Darcy," she said. "I already told you, my Mom only lets me have one friend over."

Darcy went full-on pout again.

"Look," Honey said, "from one weapons-grade pouter to another—it won't work on me."

Darcy's pout intensified. Honey thought for sure she saw tears, alligator tears, forming in Darcy's eye sockets. It was at that moment Honey knew she was standing in the presence of greatness. Darcy Diamond was one tough, and super sticky, piece of gum.

10

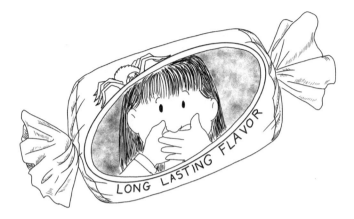

LIES, LIES, AND MORE LIES

Honey pulled open the back door, which led to the kitchen, and out bounded Half Moon, the long-haired, floppy-eared Moon family dog. He barked and wagged his tail, and then horror of horrors, he leaped on Darcy and knocked her flat on her behind onto the wet, just watered grass.

At first, Honey laughed. It was kind of funny the way Half Moon looked at Darcy. And it got even funnier when he started licking her face.

"Get him off," Darcy cried. "Get him off of me."

Honey grabbed Half's collar and pulled. "He's just saying hi," she said.

12

Claire was also laughing.

Darcy scrambled to her feet and regained her composure. "Aww, look," she said brushing her pants. "I'm all muddy." She wiped dirt from her behind.

Claire could not stop laughing. "He's done that to all of us. It's funny."

"I'm sorry," Honey said with a chuckle. "But Half thought you might be an intruder. You are a stranger. So it is kind of your fault, too."

13

Darcy patted Half's side and head. "It's okay; he can't help it. Just a big, dumb dog."

"He is not dumb." Honey said.

Darcy looked at her hands. "I'm all muddy. Can I wash my hands, please?"

"Just use the hose," Honey said. "Over there."

But that was when Harry appeared at the back door. "Honey," he said. "Don't be so rude.

Invite Darcy in to get cleaned up."

Honey let out a huge sigh. "Oh, all right."

Darcy smiled. But Honey was a little suspicious of her smile. Maybe she was just acting smug.

"Yeah," Claire, who had finally stopped laughing, said. "Invite her in. And maybe offer her milk and cookies."

14

Harry stepped aside for Darcy. "You can use the small bathroom off the kitchen."

"Thank you, Harry," she said. Then she smiled at Honey again. More smugness?

All her hard work this week of avoiding the new girl had just crumbled into dust. And Honey was not very happy about it. She just didn't have time or room in her life for one more friend, especially a friend who seemed kind of needy. But now, here was the new girl, in Honey's own house.

Honey grabbed a sack of chocolate sandwich cookies and flopped them on the table. She was not gentle. Nor was she feeling very hospitable. She felt trapped. And she did not like it. Not one ounce.

"What is her angle?" Honey said.

Claire snagged the milk carton from the fridge. "Aww, she doesn't have any angle. She's just trying really hard to be your friend."

15

"But why?" Honey said. "I have not been exactly my usual, charming and nice self."

Claire rolled her eyes.

"She must be up to something." Honey placed two cookies each on three paper towels, while Claire poured three tumblers of milk.

Darcy returned with clean hands and a wet bottom. "I think I got most of it off." She turned her butt toward Honey. "Is there much dirt left?"

"No," Honey said without looking. "You got it all."

Darcy smiled and looked around the kitchen. "You have a nice house. It's pretty much like my new house. My Dad just transferred to some tech firm in Boston, and Mom is a nurse. She got a job at the community hospital."

Honey choked on her cookie.

Claire spat her cookie across the room.

"Whaaaaaat?" Honey said. "My Mom's a nurse there, too, and my dad works at a big tech firm in Boston."

"Cool beans!" Darcy said. "I told you we were destined to be best friends. Huh, don't you think? I mean what are the odds right? We're like soul sisters. It's destiny, I say. Destiny."

Honey sighed. "I already have enough best friends. You understand, right?"

And as for destiny, Honey had never given it much thought. Destiny was something Harry talked about. Honey mostly listened to her instincts and wasn't afraid to stand up for what was right and point out what was wrong. And right now, this situation with Darcy Diamond felt wrong.

Claire raised one eyebrow—a skill Honey totally wished she could master. "It's okie dokie, fine by me," Claire said. "One more girl wouldn't matter."

Honey kicked her under the table. Claire smirked.

Darcy finished her snack. "So whatcha want to do? Play dolls or jump rope or how about a video game or Legos?"

"Sorry, Darcy," Honey said. She set her glass in the dishwasher. "But Claire and I have a project to work on."

"We do?" Claire asked.

"Yes. Remember, we're partners for that big book report?"

"Oooooooo, that's right."

"Okay," Darcy said. She placed her glass into the dishwasher. "I better go home. But let's plan on walking to school together tomorrow. We are in the same room and all, so it only makes sense. Besides it is our destiny. Remember that, Honey. You can't fight destiny."

Honey walked Darcy to the back door where they barely avoided another collision with Half Moon.

"See ya," Darcy said. "See you tomorrow. Let's meet by the headless statue in the park. It's such a cool statue. Don't you think?"

"Not especially," Honey replied. Then she closed the door.

Claire was glaring at Honey as though Honey had just broken every rule in the book. "If you were Pinocchio your nose would be six feet long."

Honey sat at the kitchen table. "I know, I

know. I lied to her—again! But she's just such a...a—"

"Buttinsky? That's what my mom would say."

"Yeah," Honey said. "A huge buttinsky."

"Yeah, but maybe you should give her a break."

"Why?" Honey asked.

19

Claire shrugged. "Maybe she is your destiny."

"Ugh, don't say that."

But as Honey looked through the back door window she felt her skin prickle. There was definitely something up with that Darcy Diamond. Maybe there was a reason she fell into Honey's life the way she did.

"Come on," Honey said, pushing that most terrible thought from her brain. "Let's go to my room."

That evening, after dinner and homework and all the chores had been finished, Honey found the best spot in the living room for television watching. Harry was in his room, as usual. Mom and Dad were in the den working on bills. And Harvest was in the den with them. So Honey felt like she practically had the whole house to herself.

She clicked the remote, put her feet on the coffee table, and was all ready to relax with a bag of chips when the doorbell rang.

"Honey," Mom called, "would you see who is at the door, please?"

"Rats!" Honey set the chips on the couch and went to the door. She pulled it opened and could not believe her eyes for a moment. "Darcy!" she said. "What are you doing here?"

"Oh, nothing. I was just out and thought I'd drop in. Isn't it fun when friends just drop by? Wanna play dolls or something?"

Honey simply stared at Darcy until she heard

her mom's voice. "Who is it, Honey?"

"Nobody, Mom. It's for me."

Darcy tried to take a step inside the house. "Listen, Darcy, I have a ton of homework and—"

"Nobody?" called Mom. "How can it be nobody?"

"It's just me, Darcy Diamond," Darcy called very loudly.

21

"Darcy Diamond?" Mom had come into the living room. "Come on in."

Honey felt her nerves start to tingle, and her brain wanted to explode. All she wanted to do was watch TV, and now she had the Princess of Annoyance in her house—again!

"Darcy," Mom said. "Are you Daisy Diamond's daughter?"

Darcy smiled. "Yes, Mrs. Moon, I am. She

works at the hospital just like you do."

Then horror of horrors, Mom draped her arm around Darcy's shoulders and walked her toward the couch. "Have a seat, dear. Your mom told me about you. She said you are Honey's age and even in the same class."

Honey sucked in a deep breath. She could not believe what was happening, right in front of her. Right in her own home. Betrayed by her own mother!

"Isn't that terrific?" Mom said. "Come on, Honey, have a seat. Visit with your new friend."

But Honey didn't budge. "I can't Mom. Tons of homework."

23

"I already did my homework," Darcy said. "It wasn't hard. I can help if you want?"

"No, no," Honey said. "I'd rather do my own homework, thank you."

"Honey," Mom said. "Don't be that way. Darcy is new to town."

Mom turned her attention back to Darcy. "So tell me, how do you like our little town?"

"Oh, it's great," Darcy said. "I just love all the spooky stuff. It's kind of funny. Dad says it's weird, but he's not gonna let it bother him. My mother isn't too thrilled about it. But I like it."

"Well, it was all Mayor Kligore's idea. He said it would put Sleepy Hollow on the map and help the businesses in town that were struggling."

24

"Oh," Darcy said. But Honey thought she wasn't all that interested in the town's history.

Ugh. Honey moved closer to her mother. "Really, Mother, I should just get to work."

Honey's mom looked into her eyes, the way she did when she was trying to figure out what Honey was really feeling. "Well, okay, Honey," Mom said. "I suppose you're right."

Honey nodded.

"It's okay," Darcy said. "We'll still walk to school together tomorrow, right?"

Honey looked at her mother who was by now looking daggers at Honey. "Sure," Honey said. "Sounds terrific. Just terrific."

Even though it wasn't terrific. It was downright terrible. Here she was trying to shake Darcy loose, and her mom was forcing them together. It was kind of like trying to add one more bowling pin to the line-up. It just wasn't right. Out of kilter. That's what Honey thought.

25

Honey walked Darcy to the door. "Thanks for coming over," Honey said even though she didn't mean it. She closed the door but did not turn around right away. Instead, she stood there, with her forehead pressed against the door. She could feel her mother breathing down her neck.

"Honey Moon," Mom said. "What was that all about? You were so incredibly rude to that girl. She's new in town and probably just wants to make friends. She seemed very nice to me, and I think she really likes you."

Honey turned around. She still couldn't look her mother in the eyes, though.

"And furthermore," Mom said. "You told me you finished your homework."

"I did," Honey said. "Right after dinner."

"Then why did you tell Darcy a lie?"

Honey stamped her foot. It wasn't that she enjoyed lying. She really didn't know why she did it. "I just did, okay?" Honey stomped across the room to the steps.

"Okay, okay, for now," Mom called. "You'll tell me when you're ready. You go think about it for a while."

Honey threw herself on her bed. The trouble was, she didn't know why Darcy rattled her cage so much. Yeah, she was annoying and talked a lot. But it wasn't like she was mean. She was not like Clarice or anything. But still, even though she should be nice to Darcy, Honey was dreading the walk to school in the morning.

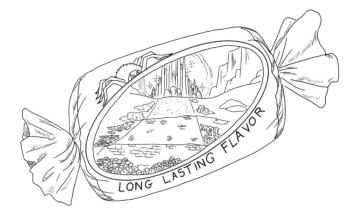

LONG LASTING FLAVOR

THE AUDITION

The next morning, Honey woke early, dressed quickly, ate breakfast like she hadn't eaten in ten days, and scooted out the door—hoping she'd miss Darcy. But no. There she was, standing next to the Headless Horseman statue.

"Honey, Honey, over here," Darcy called. "I've been waiting for you. I got here extra early so I wouldn't miss you."

Honey stopped dead in her tracks and let out a huge sigh. There was just no fighting it.

She joined Darcy at the statue.

"Good morning, Darcy," she said, but she sounded more like a customer service rep than a friend.

"Hey, Honey, this is such a cool statue. It's from that story, *The Legend of Sleepy Hollow.* Ichabod Crane and all that spooky stuff."

"Yeah, yeah, everybody knows that."

Darcy ran her hand over the horse's leg. "It's so cold. What's it made out of? Gold?"

Honey laughed. "No. It's bronze. They melted the bells that used to hang in North Church and made this stupid monstrosity with the metal."

"Oh," Darcy said. "Well, why'd they do that?"

Honey shrugged. "They just did."

"Okay," Darcy said. "So we should go to school. We have time to play on the playground first. I thought you might be early.

You seem like the early bird to me."

Honey set off toward school. "Yeah, yeah. The early bird that catches the worm."

The bell rang, and Honey headed into school with Darcy sticking to her like gum again.

"I was thinking," Darcy said. "Let's ask Mrs. Tenure if she'll let us sit next to each other. I have to sit next to that weird girl; what's her name?"

29

"Brianna. And she's not weird. She's just a little different. You'll see. You might like her."

"Okay, okay, it's just that I've never seen a girl wear a cowboy outfit to school before."

"She likes to dress up."

Darcy followed Honey into class. Honey had never been so happy to find her seat on the other side of the room from Darcy. Relief at last.

Mrs. Tenure took attendance. Darcy raised her hand, like she was reaching for the stars, when her name was called. Honey just shook her head and groaned.

"I have exciting news," Mrs. Tenure said. "It's spring musical time. This year we are doing *The Wizard of Oz.*"

Everybody cheered. Especially Honey. *Oz* was one of her favorite stories of all time. She'd seen the movie six times and read the book seven. She almost knew every part by heart.

"Ooooo, ooooo," Darcy cried. "Can I play Dorothy, please?   I would make the best Dorothy."

The whole class groaned.

"Well, perhaps, Darcy," Mrs. Tenure said. "But we have to hold auditions."

"Oh, that's just fine," Darcy said. "I excel at auditions!"

Honey gave herself a face palm.

Mrs. Tenure continued, "Auditions will be held next Tuesday after school in the café-gym-atorium. If you want a part, raise your hand, and I will hand you a script. Read and rehearse the parts you think you might like."

Nearly everyone raised their hands. There were always a few kids who could not care less about the school play. Kids like Clarice Kligore and Claire Sinclair. Clarice was always too busy being mean, and Claire thought the school play was lame. She'd rather tryout for baseball.

Honey looked at Darcy, who had just pulled a yellow highlighter pen from her desk. "All the real stars highlight their parts," Darcy said. "That's what I'm gonna do."

The class groaned.

"Do you ever stop talking?" Clarice called across the room. "Criminy, you're like a crow.

Caw, caw, caw."

"That's enough, Clarice," Mrs. Tenure said.

Honey smiled.

"Sorry," Darcy said. "I'm just excited for the play. *The Wizard of Oz* is my favorite story."

Jumpin' tiddlywinks! Honey glared at her script. Now, Darcy took her favorite story. Honey leaned over to Claire. "She'll see. I'm gonna be the best Dorothy ever!"

Honey watched the clock until lunch time. Her class lined up, with Brianna in the lead this time. Darcy followed Brianna, and Honey was perfectly fine at the back. But everything changed once they reached the cafeteria. Honey packed, but she bought milk and Fritos. She sat at her usual table with her best friends, Claire and Becky.

Becky was not in Honey's class, so she was always glad to see her at lunch.

"Honey," Becky said. "Did you get a script?"

"Yes," Honey said as she sat at the table. "I'm trying out for Dorothy."

"Oh, you'll be the best Dorothy," Becky said. "I was thinking about trying out for Glinda."

"Cool," Honey said as she unpacked her sandwich. "Just once I'd love it if Mom would pack me a normal sandwich." She glared at the cucumber and watercress sandwich. She glared even harder at the small bag of baby carrots and the tiny tub of hummus. At least she had Fritos.

33

"Maybe Clarice should be the witch," Claire said.

"Yeah, but she isn't trying out. Maybe Darcy should be the witch," Honey laughed. As she laughed, she caught Claire's eye. Darcy was standing right behind her. Honey looked over her shoulder. "Darcy. I didn't see you."

"That's okay," Darcy said. "I came to sit with

you." Darcy sat next to Honey. "I'm glad there's a space. Now we can eat together every day."

"Sure," Honey said. She felt a little bad about what she said. But not so bad that she couldn't say, "Sometimes I like to eat alone." Another lie. This was definitely getting out of control.

Darcy pulled her script out of her back pocket. "I definitely don't want to be the witch. I want to be Dorothy."

Honey swallowed her sandwich bite so hard she hurt her throat.

"But that's Honey's part," Claire said.

"Oh." Darcy dipped a chicken nugget into BBQ sauce. "Well, we still have to try out."

"I'm sure Mrs. Tenure will find a part for you, Darcy," Becky said. "Honey always gets the lead."

35

Darcy looked at her script. "I have a feeling we're not in Kansas, anymore."

Honey swallowed her next bite of watercress quickly. "That's pretty good, Darcy, but you should really practice." She dipped a carrot into the humus.

"Oh, okay," Darcy said. "Let's practice after school. I can come to your house."

Claire laughed.

Honey didn't say a word. Stay calm, Honey Moon. Stay calm.

The next few days before auditions were set to begin ended up being pretty rough days for Honey. She tried everything to avoid Darcy Diamond, but somehow Darcy always showed up. Once, Honey even hid behind the Horseman statue hoping Darcy would just walk right past her. Honey hated the stupid old statue. It gave her the creeps and made her think about Halloween, but it was worth the fright if she could hide from Darcy. But no, Darcy still found her.

She even pretended to be sick one day, but her mother would not let her get away with it. When your mom is a nurse, faking an illness is not that easy. Honey had even asked Harry if he could just make Darcy disappear.

"Put her in that box," she told Harry. "And POOF! She's gone."

"And just don't bring her back, right Honey?" Harry said.

"That's right, bro. Poof. No more Darcy."

Harry could only laugh at the suggestion, of course. "That's not my style, little sister."

But that's pretty much how the week went. Honey did manage to study her part and even memorized most of it. Unfortunately, so did Darcy. Becky studied her lines, and Claire sat around and poked fun at them, calling them drama queens and thespians.

37

And then the big day arrived. Honey was so excited that morning she couldn't even eat breakfast. But good old Mom made her eat something.

"At least eat a banana," Mom said. "You'll get sick in class."

"Okay, okay," Honey said. "One banana and maybe a waffle and some orange juice."

Mom laughed. "Sit down, Honey," she said. "I'll make you a nice breakfast, and you too, Harry."

Harry sat next to Harvest who was busy with Cheerios and yogurt.

Honey raced to school. She didn't even care that Darcy was racing at her heels. "I'm so excited, Honey," Darcy called. "Aren't you? I can't wait for school to be over. Hey, maybe Harry can speed up time."

Honey did not say a single word. She didn't want anything to spoil her concentration. Somehow, Honey managed to make it to the end of the day.

"Now, listen up," Mrs. Tenure said. "If you are trying out for *Oz* you may gather your things and head down to the café-gym-atorium. But be quiet. Classes are still going on."

Honey packed her backpack. "I'll see you later," she told Claire. Claire had to stay in the room until the bell rang.

"Right," Claire said. "Break a leg."

Honey made a stop at Becky's class. "Come

38

on," Honey said. "I want to be first in line."

"Oh, you don't have to worry. You know you'll get the part."

"I know, I know," Honey said. She pulled Becky's sleeve. "But still."

Darcy stood nearby. "I'd rather go last. That way I can size up the competition. It's best to go last. Don't you think?"

Honey and Becky headed down the hallway. "No," Honey said. "I think it's best to go first. Besides, Mrs. Fortissimo is there, and I want to get a chance to practice with the piano."

"Piano," Darcy said. "Why is there a piano?"

"Oh, you didn't know?' Honey said. "You have to sing a few bars of 'Somewhere Over the Rainbow.'"

Honey watched Darcy swallow like she was swallowing a sour apple. "Really? I...I guess I didn't see that in the script."

Honey opened her script. "Look it's right here. On the last page."

Darcy looked through her entire script. "I... I don't have that page."

"Uh, oh," Honey said. "Well, everybody knows that song. You can wing it. Wing it to sing it."

Honey and Becky sped up their pace. Darcy kept right up with them. "Well, that's okay; I have an excellent singing voice."

Honey chose not to say a word. Not a single word.

Honey and Becky dropped their backpacks against the gym wall. Mrs. Fortissimo was on the stage standing next to the piano. It was on wheels and could be rolled all over the school. Honey and Becky climbed the steps to the stage. But somehow, Darcy had made it on stage first.

40

Honey shook her head and got in line.

"Gee," Becky said. "It looks like the whole fourth and fifth grades are here."

"Yeah," Honey said. "Everyone except Claire."

"Well, Claire and the other jocks."

Mrs. Fortissimo clapped her hands, and the group quieted down. "Now listen up," she said. "When Mrs. Tenure gets here, you will all have a chance to read for the part you want, and then those with singing parts will stand next to me and sing a few bars of either 'Somewhere Over the Rainbow' or 'If I only Had a Brain.'"

41

Trevor laughed. He was standing a few people behind Honey. "Yeah, if only Noah had a brain. He'd know not to even try out."

"Okay, okay," Mrs. Fortissimo said. "No more wisecracks. We're here to work."

Honey glanced at her script. This was going to be a piece of cake.

Mrs. Fortissimo played a few, loud chords on the piano. That always quieted the group. "Honey Moon," she called. "Why don't you come up first?"

Honey smirked at Darcy, who she had to admit was looking pretty confident herself. "Okay, Mrs. F. I'd love to go first."

Mrs. F. played a short intro as Honey stood next to the piano. And then Honey sang, "Somewhere over the rainbow, bluebirds fly..." As she sang Honey felt every eye looking at her, but she did not get nervous. No, Honey sang six bars beautifully. Everyone applauded when she had finished. Even Claire who was sitting in the audience. Honey caught her eye, and Claire gave her thumbs-up.

"Very good, Honey," Mrs. F said.

Paige and Wendy went next. Honey thought they did all right. And then it was Darcy's turn. Honey took a deep breath as Darcy marched toward the piano. She took an even deeper

42

breath and let it out through her nose like a bull when Darcy smiled into the waiting crowd. But first, Mrs. Fortissimo made Darcy spit out her gum.

Mrs. F. played the intro and then Darcy sang, "Somewheeeereeeeee over the rainbowwwwwwww."

But it did not sound nice. In fact, Darcy's

43

voice sounded more like the screeches and hollers of crows fighting with a cat or the sometimes eerie sounds that came from Folly Farm. Some kids in the group laughed. But Darcy did not seem to care; she just kept on singing, even after Mrs. F. stopped playing the piano. Tone deaf. Darcy Diamond was completely tone deaf, and she didn't even know it.

"Thank you," Mrs. F said, interrupting the screeching. "That's enough, Darcy."

Darcy smiled at the snickering crowd. Honey felt her heart sink. Now what? A strange feeling bubbled up in Honey's stomach, and it wasn't today's watercress and cucumbers. No, Honey felt sorry for Darcy.

A look washed over Darcy's face. She turned bright red. Honey thought she saw Darcy sneak a swipe at her eyes that were probably filling with tears.

"Quiet down, everyone," Mrs. F called. Then she slammed the piano keys with a terrible clash of notes that sounded worse than Darcy's singing voice. Darcy still tried to smile. Then she turned to Mrs. F and said, "Oh, I just remembered. I can't be in the play. My mother needs me to...to take care of my little sister after school." Darcy grabbed her backpack from the pile and ran out so fast she was a blur.

Honey looked out at Claire. Claire shrugged.

"That girl sings worse than a raven with its feathers caught in an elevator door," Trevor said.

45

"Yeah," Noah said. "Can't she hear how bad she is?"

"Right," Honey said. "She was...was pretty awful." Except, rats of all rats, Honey's heart toward Darcy had started to grow. Now what? Destiny?

46

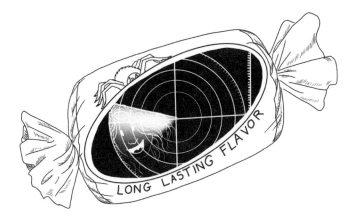

DARCY STAYS FOR SUPPER

After auditions, Honey, Becky, and Claire stopped at Spooky Sweets. But Honey was not that hungry. She only got three caramel brains. Claire loaded down on Gruesome Gummies. And Becky couldn't choose between Mummy Mints or Chocolate Spiders. Honey made the choice for her.

"Get the mints," Honey said. "Geeze. It's candy, not exactly a life and death decision."

Honey stomped out of the shop and

crammed the brains into her mouth. She chewed hard.

"Hey," Becky said when she came out of the store. "What's your problem?"

"Yeah," Claire mumbled as she pried a gummy goon from her front teeth. "You definitely got the part. You always get the best parts. You're like the Tina Fey of Sleepy Hollow."

48

That made Honey smile. "I...I just feel weird. Okay?"

"Sick, weird?" Becky asked.

"Are you gonna puke?" Claire asked. "Don't do it in front of me."

"No," Honey replied. "I'm not sick. I just want to be alone."

"Okay," Becky said.

"Yeah, sure thing," Claire said. "We'll leave you alone. Geeze."

Honey waited until Claire and Becky had turned onto Maple Street. She hiked her turtle backpack higher on her shoulders and set off toward home—the long way, past the church, past the statue, and past Folly Farm where the Kligore's lived. The place gave her the creeps, but she thought maybe a few creeps would help get rid of the other feelings inside. Feelings that made her sad for being mean to Darcy. For laughing when Half Moon pushed Darcy into the mud and she fell on her butt, and she felt bad for lying.

49

The day was warm, and the ever-present aroma of pumpkin spice and nutmeg and burning leaves wafted through the air. Honey took a deep breath and headed into the Town Green. Sleepy Hollow was not your ordinary small town. Where most towns had a statue of a war hero or founding father, Sleepy Hollow had that infernal statue of the Headless Horseman. It was all part of the touristy stuff that Mayor Kligore set in motion a long time ago—before Honey was even born. It was Kligore's idea to turn Sleepy Hollow into Spooky Town. And people loved it.

But not Honey, not so much anyway. As she walked toward the statue she tried to muster her bravery—after all, she really was a very brave girl—like Pippi Longstocking. And as

50

much as she hated to admit it, she was kind of hoping Darcy might be hiding behind Old Creepy Horse.

Darcy was not there, but Honey did hear a voice.

"Honey? What's wrong?"

Honey looked around, but she didn't see anyone.

"Honey? Look for me. I'm here."

Now the voice sounded like it was coming from her backpack. Honey shrugged the despicable turtle from her back. "What do you want?"

"I want what you want."

Honey sat on the grass. "Seriously? You want to stop feeling sad and be glad about getting the Dorothy part?"

"Yes."

51

Honey felt her stomach churn. This was getting weird. Ever since she got the ugliest, turtle-shaped backpack in the world as a Christmas present, she knew it wasn't ordinary. But this was definitely weird.

Harry had Rabbit. And now, it seemed, that Honey had Turtle.

Honey gave herself a face palm. "Turtle?"

52

"You need to make this right."

"I know. But how? Harry has magic. What do I have?"

"Radar."

"Radar?" Honey thought a moment. It was true. She always got a sinking feeling when things were not quite right. Usually, she knew to steer clear of the statue and Folly Farm, and when Harry was off fighting evil with Good Mischief Team, she always cheered him on.

But now Darcy was the brightest blip on her

radar screen.

"Thanks, Turtle," Honey said. She slipped the bag over her shoulders. "But please, please, please do not tell anyone I talk to you."

"Don't worry, Honey. I got you covered."

As Honey walked on toward home, it actually started to feel strange that Darcy was not on her heels. She must have really gotten her feelings hurt when the kids laughed. There was still an hour to go before dinner when Honey got home. Honey saw Mom's minivan in the driveway.

53

Honey pushed open the front door. "Mom!" she called. "What's for dinner?"

"Honey," Mom said from the kitchen. "Come in here."

"Okay." Honey slipped Turtle from her shoulders. "Now, stay cool. No talking."

"Mom," Honey said. "I tried out for...for..." She stopped.

"Hi, Honey," Mom said. "Look who came for a visit. Darcy. We were just having a nice chat."

"And some really good zucchini and carob cookies," Darcy said.

"Oh, cool," Honey said. But in that moment her growing heart shrunk again. "What are you doing here?" Honey tossed her backpack into the living room. She thought she heard Turtle say, "Ouch."

"Honey," Mom said. "Don't be rude. She came to see if you wanted to play. But you were so late from school I invited her for a snack."

"Yeah, my mom is on night shift."

"So Darcy is staying for supper," Mom said.

Honey grabbed a cookie and sat at the table. "That's great. Happy you can stay." But

54

she didn't mean it and just when she resolved to not lie anymore out came a whopper.

"Now look," Mom said. "I ordered pizza, and I'll throw together a salad. Harry should be home soon. Dad has a meeting, and Harvest doesn't seem to be feeling well."

"Oh," Honey said. "Pizza?"

"I know, I know, but I'm really too tired to cook and pizza every once in a while won't hurt us. It's Hawaiian. So you get a serving of fruit. Now you two set the table—the dining room table. Pizza will be here in just a few minutes."

"Okay, Mrs. Moon," Darcy said. "And thank you soooooo much for inviting me. I just love pizza...oh, and salad too, of course."

Honey shook her head. What was she worried about? Darcy was perfectly fine. It was like the auditions never happened. Except they did, and Honey wanted to tell Mom that she probably got the part of Dorothy. But maybe Darcy already told her. No. Mom would have said something.

The doorbell rang, and Mom ran to get the pizzas. Harry burst through the back door.

"I saw the pizza guy," he said. "We're actually having pizza for dinner? What gives?"

"I know, right," Honey said. "Mom is off her rocker or something."

"I am not off my rocker," Mom said. She set the pizzas on the dining room table. "I just had a hard day, and I don't feel like cooking."

"Yes," Darcy said. "And your father is working late, and Harvest is sick."

Honey shot Harry a look.

"Okay, then," Harry said. "Let's eat. I'm starved."

"Me, too," Darcy said.

Honey took her seat. "I tried out for Dorothy today."

"Oh, yes," Mom said. "Darcy said you did really well. She said you have a great singing voice."

Honey looked at Darcy. "She did?"

"Yes," Darcy said. "It's true. I can't sing a note."

Now Honey was in kind of a pickle. She didn't know if Darcy told her about her own disastrous tryout, and she didn't want to say anything that would embarrass Darcy anymore. But she didn't have to.

"I tried out, too," Darcy said. She was speaking to Harry.

58

"That's cool," Harry said as he chewed. "What part didja get?"

Darcy looked at her paper plate and picked at a pepperoni. "Oh, my audition wasn't so good."

Honey practically spat cheese and a pineapple chunk clear across the room. Not good?

Her voice nearly shattered the stage lights and all she could say was, 'not good'? Honey bit her tongue.

"We can't all be great at everything," Mom said. "I'm sure you'll find the right club or activity at school, Darcy."

"You were a pretty good magician's assistant," Harry said.

"Hey," Mom said. "I'm sure Honey can help you find just the right thing. Can't you, Honey? Take Darcy under your wing so to speak. Honey knows everything there is to know about Sleepy Hollow Elementary."

Honey swallowed. No. This couldn't be happening. She glared at Mom. But even though Turtle was face down on the living room carpet she felt his presence. "Sure, Mom." But once again, Honey's heart was just not in it.

60

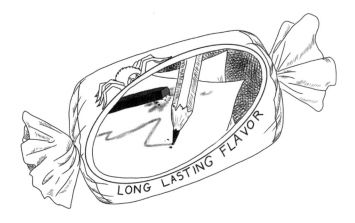

ART CLUB

Honey went to bed that night dreading the next day. It was like Darcy Diamond was now permanently stuck to her shoe. She couldn't tell Mom she didn't want to help Darcy find the right club, and Harry wasn't exactly making it any better.

She looked over at Turtle. The backpack was on her desk chair. "You know this is your fault."

"My fault?"

"Yeah. You got me all confused. I was

perfectly fine trying to keep Darcy Diamond a million miles away from me, but you got me thinking that even though I don't want to, I should help her."

"Me? Now how could I do that?"

"By getting into my heart and mind and stuff."

"Oh, so you care about her now, and that's a bad thing?"

Honey looked at the ceiling. "No. Of course not."

Honey waited for Turtle's response. But none came. "Great. So now I get to figure this out all by myself. How on earth can I get the stickiest piece of chewing gum off my shoe?"

But the more she thought, the clearer it all became. Maybe getting Darcy into a new club was just the right thing to do. Maybe then, she'd make a new friend.

Morning came, and Honey dressed for school. It was Friday, and all the girls wore their spirit socks on Fridays—orange and black striped knee-highs. She wore a black skirt and orange top and looked at herself in the mirror. "Good old Sleepy Hollow."

After gagging down one of Mom's breakfast smoothies, Honey ran off to school. She usually met up with Claire and Becky and today was no different, except when they reached the Horrible Horseman, Darcy was waiting.

"Hi. Good morning," she called.

Honey waved. "Morning." Be nice Honey Moon. Be nice. You have a plan. Darcy Diamond's destiny was definitely a new club.

"Hey," Becky called. Then she turned to Honey and said, "She doesn't look sad or anything about yesterday."

"She's not," Honey said. "It's like her emotions are encased in steel. Nothing bothers that girl."

"Hi," Claire said. "Too bad about the singing and stuff."

Darcy smiled and looked away. "Oh, I don't care. So I can't sing. I can do other things better. Honey is gonna help me find just the right club."

Honey looked at Becky. "Hey," Honey said. "How about art club? Becky is a great artist. You can go with her."

"Art club?" Darcy said. "That sounds fun. I love to draw and paint. Is it easy to join? Will I get to draw and paint and stuff?"

"Sure, we do all that stuff," Becky said as the girls headed toward school. "We meet in the art room right after school every Friday."

Honey, Becky, and Claire walked on without saying much of anything. Claire kept tossing a softball in the air and catching it. Honey kept thinking she heard Turtle, and Becky never really did talk much. But that was not the case for Darcy.

"I love art," she said. "Will we get to paint or sculpt with clay? What about paper-mache or oil paints? Do we do much drawing? I love to draw. Especially horses. Hey, maybe I can draw the Horseman or maybe the school raven."

Honey kept shaking her head. How could anyone talk so much?

"Hey," Darcy said. "You guys are all wearing the same socks. Why are you wearing the same socks?"

"It's spirit day," Honey said. "All the girls wear their spirit socks on Fridays."

"Oh, I don't have spirit socks. Where do I get them? Can I buy them today?"

Honey stopped walking. "NO!" she said louder than she had meant to. "You can only buy them at the school store, and it's only open every other Wednesday. And can you please stop asking so many questions?!" The words shot out of her mouth like tennis balls from an automatic server gone haywire.

"Oh," Darcy said. "Okay."

Honey walked ahead. "Patience," Turtle said.

"I know." Honey hitched her backpack higher on her shoulders. Hopefully, now, she was close to getting Darcy off her back.

School did not go well. Mrs. Tenure caught Honey staring out the window, lost in a daydream. But it wasn't a daydream. It was a serious case of what Honey's dad called "the guilties." Honey didn't want to feel bad about spouting off at Darcy. But she did.

And later that day during PE it wasn't Darcy the kids laughed at. It was Honey when she got so distracted that Clarice Kligore tripped her during the crab walk races. But at least the day was nearly over, and now Darcy would be Becky's problem. At least now she could catch a break.

The bell rang, and Honey gathered her books.

"So should I just meet Becky in the art room or go to her classroom?" Darcy asked Honey.

"Go to her classroom. You can walk together." Honey slipped her backpack over her shoulders.

"Will you come too?" Darcy asked. "You don't have play practice. Please, Honey. Please come to art club."

"No. I'm not in art club. That's Becky's club." Honey felt the pressure of Turtle on her back.

"Please," Darcy whined. "Please come with me. At least walk with me. I don't know Becky like I know you."

Honey took a deep breath like she was about to jump into the deep end of the pool. "Okay. If you really want me."

"You are my best friend," Darcy said. "It's our destiny, remember?"

Honey let out a long sigh.

Becky was waiting at her classroom. "Great," Becky said. "I'm glad you're still coming, Darcy."

"And so is Honey," Darcy said.

Becky looked at Honey. "Really? But you never wanted to come to art club before."

"I'm just walking to the art room." Honey sighed.

The art room was not very crowded. Honey counted seven students and Miss Pallet, the art teacher.

Miss Pallet clapped her hands. "Okay, okay. I see we have two new club members today. I know you Honey Moon, but who is your friend?"

Honey cringed. "Darcy. Darcy Diamond. She's new to Sleepy Hollow."

"Welcome, Darcy."

Honey could feel Darcy's big smile. But she didn't even look at her. Honey picked up Turtle and started to walk away.

"Where are you going?" Miss Pallet asked.

"Oh, I just came to introduce Darcy."

"Stay," Miss Pallet said. "You might enjoy it."

69

Honey shook her head and took a seat. Darcy smiled and clapped. Becky leaned over and said, "This should be interesting."

"So today," Miss Pallet said, "we are going to finish up our self-portraits. Honey and Darcy, you two can get yours started. Becky will show you the materials we are using."

"So just get a piece of the large white paper over there," Becky said, "and you can use charcoal or pencil."

"No colors?" Darcy said.

"Not this time," Becky said.

Honey and Darcy found the large white paper.

"So I have a question," Honey asked Becky. "How are we supposed to draw our faces if we can't see them?"

Becky laughed. "Oh, yeah. I forgot to tell you. You have to do it from memory. Or from feeling your face. Here's mine."

Becky held up her picture.

"Wow," Darcy said. "That's really good. It's almost as good as if you took it on your iPhone."

Honey shook her head and started to draw. She chose charcoal. Darcy chose pencil.

"Hey, that's pretty good, Honey," Miss Pallet said a little while later. "Good proportions and good perspective. Excellent work."

Honey looked at her drawing. She felt pretty good about it.

"I wonder how Darcy is doing?" Becky asked.

Darcy had taken her paper to the other side of the room. She was sitting in the corner, all hunched over.

"Let's go see," Honey said.

But Miss Pallet got to Darcy first. "Come on, Darcy," Miss Pallet said. "Show us your portrait."

Honey and Darcy locked eyes when Darcy stood. "Here I am!" she said with a huge smile. She held up her drawing so the whole club could see. Honey gasped. So did Becky. A few of the other kids tried not laugh, but one big guy couldn't help it and let out a loud laugh. Miss Pallet quieted him and the others down.

12

Honey couldn't take her eyes off Darcy's drawing. It was pretty awful. Darcy's face looked more like a pancake with raisin eyes. Her nose was melty, and her ears reminded Honey of cat ears. She even heard the big guy say, "All she needs is whiskers."

But Darcy looked so pleased with it, until Miss Pallet said, "That's a fine effort Darcy, but... but you might just need a little work on the nose and eyes and—"

"Everything!" shouted Clarice.

"Oh, no!" Honey said. She hadn't seen Clarice

earlier. "I didn't know she was in the club."

"Yes," Becky said. "She's pretty good."

"Your drawing looks like it was drawn by a two-year-old," Clarice said.

"That's not helpful, Clarice," Miss Pallet said. "Constructive criticism works best."

Darcy just laughed like she was joining in with everyone else. "That's how I meant to draw it."

73

But Honey did not believe her.

Miss Pallet smiled at Darcy. "Of course you did. It's a fine effort."

That was when Darcy looked at the clock and said, "Oh, I better go. I'm gonna be late." She grabbed her backpack and ran out of the room. But first, she crammed a piece of gum in her mouth.

Honey looked at Darcy's drawing. It was

pretty terrible. In normal art class, it would have been okay. But this was art club. People were expected to do better.

"Too bad," Becky said. "She really isn't a very good artist."

Honey sat at Becky's table. "I know. She isn't very good at anything. Except talking."

"If only we had a club for talkers."

THE VANISHING GIRL

Saturday morning arrived with bright sun and a slight breeze puffing the window curtains. Honey was thrilled that the week was over, and she could have a couple of days to relax and not deal with Darcy Diamond. She stayed in bed a little longer and thought about all the things she could do. She could hang out with Becky and Claire. They had been talking about exploring the Sleepy Hollow Cemetery. Or they could go shopping on Shopper's Row.

"That's it," Honey said as she climbed out of bed. She had some leftover birthday money and maybe, just maybe Mom would add a little to it, and she could buy the new shirt she saw in Skeleton's Closet BooTique—the most chic dress shop in Sleepy Hollow.

As Honey got dressed, she thought of other things to fill her Saturday. She definitely wanted to go to the Learned Owl Bookstore. It was one of her favorite places on the entire planet. Mr. Pendergrass, the owner, didn't mind if folks hung out and read books or talked.

Honey reached inside her backpack. She found an extra dollar and sixty-seven cents. The rest of her cash was in a jar on her dresser. After counting out thirty-two dollars, she shoved the money in her pocket. Then she checked her hair in the mirror. "Perfect." She moved her head so her ponytail bounced. "Just the right amount." She smiled at her reflection. "This is going to be the best day ever!"

"It's always best to be prepared."

Honey caught sight of Turtle in the mirror. She blinked, hoping he would disappear. But Honey knew the thing about special backpacks is that they stick around. Once you have a Turtle in your life—it's there to stay.

"Prepared?" Honey said. "I got my money. My hair is perfect today. I'm wearing my favorite jeans and best of all, no Darcy Diamond."

"It's just that destiny has a way of sneaking up on you."

11

Honey turned. "Look, Turtle, I get the feeling you are trying to tell me something. I think I know what it is, but please, I need a day off from Darcy Diamond, the Endless Talker."

Honey waited. But Turtle said nothing.

"Well, good," Honey said. "Then it's settled. I get to spend time with my true best friend, Becky." She grabbed the backpack and stared into its googly eyes. "Destiny? That's the stuff Mom and Harry are always yakking about. I just want to be a kid."

"A kid with a purpose. A kid with radar."

Honey squinted at Turtle. "You think you're so smart."

Mom had Honey's breakfast already on the table.

"Yogurt and granola," she said.

"Yummy," Honey said. "Is it peach?"

"Yep," Mom said. "With the little chunks."

Honey was not crazy about all of Mom's healthy choices, but peach yogurt with granola was one Honey enjoyed. "This day is starting out great!"

Mom sat at the table with a cup of coffee. "I'm having a good morning, too. Dad took Harvest to the park already, and Harry is getting ready for his magic show. He's performing at Nellie Grim's party."

"Great," Honey said. "Everything is great today."

Harry stuck his head through the back door. "Hey, Mom, I'll be in the garage. Let me know when Darcy gets here."

Honey dropped her spoon on the floor, which riled Half Moon. He grabbed the spoon and dashed out the kitchen door, nearly knocking Harry over.

79

"Oh, no," Mom said. "He's going to bury another spoon. Catch him, Harry."

"Hold on," Honey hollered. "What's this about Darcy?"

Harry grinned. "She's helping me with my act today. Just like before, remember? With my 'Vanishing Girl' trick."

Another face palm for Honey. But then she perked up. "But, that means she'll be with you, not me. Cool."

"Right," Harry said. He looked at Honey with squinty eyes. "I don't get the big deal. She's a cool kid."

"Fine. Fine," Honey said, "I'm outta here."

"Not so fast, young lady," Mom said. "Mind letting me on your Saturday plans?"

Honey brought her bowl to the sink. She rinsed it and set it in the dishwasher. Her spoon had, of course, run off with the dog. "Becky and I are going shopping. I saw a new shirt I want, and then we are going to the bookstore and then probably a stop at Spooky Sweets."

"That sounds very nice," Mom said.

Honey put her arms around her mother and kissed her cheek. "But, Mom, I was wondering if you could add a little cash to my stash."

"Whaaaaaat?" Mom said. "I thought you had birthday money."

"I do, but I could use a little more, just to be sure. Please, Mom. I'll do extra chores."

"Okay, go get my bag. It's in the living room."

"You are the best mom ever!" Honey said.

She had just grabbed her mother's handbag when the doorbell rang.

"Rats!" Honey said. "I bet it's Darcy."

Honey decided to ignore the bell and headed back to the kitchen, but she didn't make it.

"Honey," Mom called. "Get the door, please."

"Double rats!"

Honey opened the door, and there she stood. Darcy Diamond all dressed up in a magician's assistant outfit—which was really just a purple tunic top pulled over black tights. And she wore a red velvet cape that looked like she had made it herself. The sewing was crooked. It was way too big, and it looked like Darcy had tried to sew a giant 'H' on it. But it looked more like a crazy stick figure.

"Hi Honey," Darcy said. "I'm sorry we can't play today. I'm helping Harry with his magic show. I can't wait to vanish again. Of course, I know the secret, but I'm sworn to secrecy. I can't tell you. Even though we are best friends, and we have destiny and all."

Honey raised her hand. "Cool, Darcy." Honey took a deep breath. She didn't want to say anything that could jeopardize her most perfect Saturday plans.

"Harry is in the garage. He said to meet him there."

"Okay," Darcy said. "I should just go through the house. That would be easier, wouldn't it? And I can say hi to your mom. She's the best."

Honey stepped to the side and let Darcy into the house. "Go ahead. Mom's in the kitchen."

83

Darcy followed Honey.

"Darcy, good morning," Mom said. "Harry's in the garage."

"I already told her, Mom," Honey said.

"That's fine, dear," Mom said. Then Mom said something that struck horror in Honey's heart. Words that Honey did not want to hear.

"Hey, I have a thought. Harry's magic show

will be over at noon. Maybe Darcy can meet you at the BooTique."

Honey thought her heart would pound right out of her chest.

"Oh, really? That sounds terrific. I'm sure my mom will let me."

"Okay," Mom said. "Harry is waiting for you, Darcy."

Darcy headed out the door with Half Moon following close behind.

Honey stamped her foot. "Mooooooommmm, why did you do that?"

Mom pulled her wallet from her bag. "Do what?"

"Invite Darcy to ruin my day. I didn't want her to come. Don't you get it? I can't stand *THAT GIRL!*"

But then Honey saw her mother's eyes grow wide.

Honey swallowed. "She's standing right behind me, right?"

Mom nodded.

Now Honey wanted to be the Vanishing Girl.

85

86

SHOPPER'S ROW

"I'm sorry, Darcy," Honey said as she turned around. "I didn't mean that."

Darcy pouted. A major-league, all-time, best-ever pout.

All Honey could do was swallow. She could feel her mother's eyes boring into her like a mining drill. "I'm sorry," she said again.

But then Darcy perked up. She didn't say a word to Honey. Just Honey's mom. "Harry asked me to come in and get his magic top hat. He said you would know where it is."

"Oh, yes, it's in the den, dear."

"Thank you," Darcy said.

Honey stamped her foot on the floor again. But this time she did not speak as loud. "It's incredible. Nothing bothers her. Nothing."

"Honey," Mom said. "I seriously doubt that's the point here. You were quite rude."

"But, Mom. It's the truth. Darcy just sticks to me. Wherever I go, she's there. I just need a break from her."

"But I thought you were helping her to fit in. Find a club or something."

"I am," Honey said. "But so far it's been a disaster. Art club was a train wreck. Harvest draws better than her. She is totally tone deaf, and all the kids laugh at her. All she can do is talk."

"I doubt that." Mom pressed some cash into Honey's palm. "Make sure the shirt fits well. And please, Honey, be careful with your words. And before you go, you owe someone an apology."

Darcy returned with the hat. "I can hardly believe I am standing here holding Harry Moon's magic top hat. I heard about his fancy rabbit tricks. I hope he performs one at the party today and—" She took a deep breath. "Don't worry, Honey, I won't bother you today."

89

Honey's shoulders drooped. Ugh. Now what should she do?

"I'm really sorry you heard me," Honey said. "But listen, I have your cell just in case. I'll text you when we get to the candy store later, and well, I really am sorry."

"Sure," Darcy said. "It's okay. We can start over."

"Oh, and Darcy," Honey said. "Harry's rabbit has a way of showing up. He's kind of always around."

"Cool beans," Darcy said. "I can't wait to see him."

"But only if Harry reveals him."

Darcy screwed up her mouth like she was thinking really, really hard. "Wow. Harry is a real magician, huh."

90

Honey pocketed the extra cash. "I forgot something."

Honey dashed up the stairs and into her room. She grabbed her turtle backpack and looked into the turtle's googly eyes. "I know we don't have school, but I have a feeling I should keep you close today." She slipped it onto her back.

"Today and every day," Turtle said.

"Yeah. I guess I'm glad you got me covered."

"We can't go wrong when we're together."

Honey jumped down the steps and headed out the front door. Usually, she took the back door, but she kind of wanted to bypass seeing Darcy if she could. That really was quite a blunder. But this time she wasn't sure if she was more upset because Darcy heard her say those mean things or because Darcy was upset and standing up for herself. It was like her radar was going in circles. First, it pointed at Darcy, but now it was quite possible she was the biggest blip on the screen.

91

She caught up with Becky at the Town Green clock tower. It was often their meeting place.

"Honey," Becky called. "I was worried you couldn't come."

"Sorry," Honey said. "But you know who came over and I...well, let's just say it took me a little longer to get out the door."

"Darcy?" Becky said. She started walking

across the park.

"Yeah," Honey said. "Get this. She's going to be Harry's assistant at his magic act today."

"Oh, that's nice." Becky picked up an acorn. "Aren't these so cool. They look like little faces with hats."

"And that is exactly why you are an artist. You notice junk like that." Honey grabbed the acorn from Becky. "I just see an acorn. A future oak tree."

Becky laughed a little. "And that's what makes you, you."

"What's that?"

"You are always thinking ahead. About the future and about possibilities."

"Well, my favorite poet, Emily Dickinson, says, 'Dwell in possibility.'" Honey said.

Becky and Honey headed onto Main Street.

"So you're an artist, and I'm a positive thinker. If I could just figure out what Darcy is good at."

"Yeah. It's been a disaster so far," Becky said.

"The only thing we know for sure is that she can talk."

"And talk and talk and ask questions," Becky said. "I'm surprised she can even do Harry's magic show."

93

Honey walked a few more paces. "Hey, let's go watch. See how she does after we're done shopping. Maybe cheer her on."

"Now that, Honey Moon, is definitely some good thinking."

"Harry is at Nellie Grims," Honey said. "Which is perfect because she lives right behind Shopper's Row."

"Let's go," Becky said. "We should have

time to go to the BooTique first."

"And then the bookstore. I want to grab the new Daisy Dolphin book."

As Honey and Becky headed toward Shopper's Row, Honey could feel Turtle on her back. She heard a whispered voice. "Way to listen to your heart."

"I go where I am needed," Honey said.

The BooTique was one of Honey's favorite shops in Sleepy Hollow. The owner, Sally Duright was young and pretty, and she always made good suggestions to girls who didn't quite know what they wanted. But that was not the case today. Honey knew exactly which blouse she wanted.

"The purple one, in the window," she told Sally. "It's so pretty and will look great with my new striped skirt."

"Oh, yeah," Becky said. "I love that skirt."

Sally brought Honey the blouse. "It's lovely," she said. "And I'm certain it will look just lovely on you."

Honey stepped into the dressing room and changed into the new blouse. That was when she noticed something she hadn't quite noticed before. It's time she talked to her mom about getting a training bra.

Becky whispered the same thing to her when she stepped out. "It's pretty," Becky said. "But...well, you know."

"You can always wear a tank or a camisole," Sally said.

Honey felt a little sad and embarrassed. She folded her arms across her chest. The blouse was lovely, just as Sally said, but now it appeared her clothes were becoming a little more complicated.

"I'll buy it," she said.

"And talk to your Mom," Becky said. "It's

no big deal."

Honey stood at the counter as Sally entered the transaction on the register. "I'm just glad Claire isn't here," Honey said. "She'd probably laugh and say something stupid."

Embarrassing things happen to everyone—even Honey Moon. But she wasn't going to let that stop her from buying the blouse.

Becky said, "Awww, it's gonna happen to her, too."

"Let's get to the bookstore," Honey said.

The Learned Owl was only three stores down from the BooTique. It was an incredible little shop. Every wall was stacked high with books. They sold everything from books to stationery and even literary socks and mugs. It was where Honey got her favorite poster.

Honey took a step through the door and took a deep breath. "Ahhhh, nothing like the smell of fresh books." Then she stood there.

"Imagine it, Becky. There must be a million stories here. Doesn't that just blow your mind?"

"Sure does," Becky said.

Honey found the title she wanted and was waiting at the counter to pay when a poster on the Community Bulletin Board caught her eye.

Keynotes for Kids!
Learn the art of professional speaking.
For students in Grades 3-8
First Meeting
Old North Church
Enter our Orator's Speech-Off Contest!

Honey stepped away to get a closer look. "Uhm. This looks interesting."

"Yeah," Becky said. "I guess, but public speaking is scary."

"I know," Honey said. "Mrs. Tenure says it's the one thing people are most frightened about—having to speak in front of an audience."

"It's hard for me," Becky said. "I get all hot, my palms sweat, and my heart pounds right out of my chest—literally."

"Seriously, Becky, if that was literal you'd be dead."

"Well, you know what I mean."

Honey checked her phone. "We should pay for our books and get over to Nellie's."

"Right," Becky said. "But do we have time to stop at Saywells? I wanted to pick up a pack of ponytail holders."

"Oh, sure. I could use some, too. But we have to make it a quick stop."

Saywells was pretty crowded. It always is on Saturdays. It was an old-fashioned drug store where you could still get breakfast and ice cream sodas. Honey and her family came to Saywells pretty much every Sunday after church. Sometimes it was the best part of going to church.

"Hey," Honey said. "Let's get a soda. We have time."

"Good idea," Becky said.

Honey and Becky sat at the Saywells counter sipping their ice cream sodas. "Saturdays are the best," Honey said.

"Especially when you have a little cash to spend."

"Yeah," Honey said. "And I'm just about empty."

"Me too," Becky said. "But it was still fun."

Honey sipped her straw, but a big chunk of ice cream would not quite make it through. So she chose to pull the straw out and use it like a spoon. Somehow, that made an already excellent ice cream soda even better.

"Do you think Darcy will do okay today?" Becky asked.

"Sure. And even if she doesn't it won't matter. That girl never gets rattled. At least not for long. She's like a human rubber band. You can stretch her, and she always bounces back."

"But even rubber bands snap," Becky said.

"Not Darcy. At least I don't think so."

"Yeah," Becky said. "She'll be fine."

Honey finished her soda and hoisted Turtle over her shoulders. "Come on. Let's go check out the show."

Nellie's house was only a couple of blocks away from Shopper's Row on Web Drive. She lived in one of the new houses being built by Mayor Kligore's We Drive By Night Company. Just the thought made Honey cringe. The houses looked fine, but Honey was suspicious of anything the mayor did—whether it was new houses or new statues or even a community picnic.

101

Honey heard the kids in the backyard.

"Come on, Becky," she said. "Let's go. We can stand in the back and watch."

Becky followed Honey. "Okay, but I hope we don't distract Darcy."

"No problem," Honey said. "Like I said, nothing bothers that girl, and besides, she'll be in Harry's Vanishing Box."

Honey and Becky found a spot under a large, spreading oak tree. "This is perfect," Honey said. "We can watch, and I'm sure she'll never notice us."

"Right," Becky said. "But say, Honey, do you know how that vanishing trick works?"

Honey laughed a little. She slipped her backpack off and let it rest against the tree trunk. "Nope. Harry doesn't tell anyone how any of the tricks are done. He says a magician never reveals his secrets."

"But Darcy has to know, right?"

Honey looked out over the small crowd of kids to the makeshift stage Harry built. "Oh, she knows just enough to make the trick work, but I bet there are things even she doesn't know."

"Shhhhhh," Becky said. "Here comes Harry."

Harry was quick to delight the audience with a few sleight of hand tricks, but when he brought out the large Vanishing Box the kids all cheered. Next, he introduced Darcy. She walked out from behind a blue velvet curtain. She wore a cape like Harry's. Harry took her hand, and they both bowed.

"And now," Harry said. "My assistant, Darcy, will step into the box."

Darcy raised her hands and waved at the kids. They all cheered. She stepped into the box, and Harry closed the door.

103

He said a few words that Honey could barely hear, and then in a loud voice, he said, "ABRACADABRA! DISAPPEAR!"

Harry turned the box three times. Then he tapped the box three times and pulled open the door, but instead of cheers, there was laughter and groans.

Darcy did not disappear. She was standing right there.

"Oh, no," Honey said. "It didn't work. Something must have gone wrong."

Harry laughed. "Sometimes this trick takes a little more magic."

Just before Harry closed the door, Honey and Darcy locked eyeballs. Harry turned the box three times, tapped the box with his magic wand three times, and pulled open the door. This time Darcy was gone.

104

The kids all cheered. And so did Honey and Becky.

"And now," Harry said. "I will bring my lovely assistant back from the far reaches of the Other World."

He spun the box three times. He tapped the box three times and shouted, "ABRACADABRA! RETURN!"

Harry pulled open the door. "Ta Daaaaa!" he said.

But the crowd gasped. Honey gasped. Darcy was not standing in the box like she was supposed to be. Darcy was gone! All that was left was her cape.

105

106

WHERE'S DARCY?

Harry closed the Vanishing Box door and moved on to more sleight of hand tricks. He tried his best to recover even though some of the kids were shouting, "Where's Darcy? Where's Darcy?"

One kid even cried and cried, and Nellie's mom had to come get her.

It was a true disaster for Harry. And worst of all, no one knew what happened to Darcy.

"Wow," Becky said. "Your brother might not know how strong his own magic is."

Honey did not know what to say. She wanted to run on stage and look for Darcy. She wanted to go be with Harry. But when she looked at Turtle and his googly eyes she knew that would be the worst thing for her to do. So she waited until Harry was finally able to end his show, and Nellie's mom invited the children inside for cake and ice cream.

Honey got to Harry as quickly as her feet could carry her.

"What happened?" she asked.

Harry looked dumbfounded. "I have no idea. She knows the trick. We practiced it. She just ran off."

"But why?" Honey asked.

"Probably because of the mistake the first time Harry said the magic words," Becky said.

Honey stepped inside the box. She tapped all the walls. She called for Darcy. "Darcy, it's okay. Come back."

But no Darcy.

"It doesn't make sense. Nothing bothers Darcy. She always bounces back."

"Well she's not here," Harry said. "That's for sure."

"Unless you really did make her disappear, and she's stuck in some in-between place," Becky said.

Harry shook his head as he gathered his props. "Impossible. It's an easy trick. It's just a trick."

"Well, some trick, Harry Moon," shouted Honey. "You lost our friend."

Honey couldn't help but notice the look on Harry's face. He was disappointed and maybe even embarrassed.

"It's not your fault, bro," Honey said. "Darcy keeps trying different things, and nothing seems to go right. Everything she tries turns into a disaster."

"I guess so," Harry said. "I just don't get it. She did the trick perfectly at rehearsal. I'll help you look for her."

Honey grabbed Becky's hand. "Come on. We better search. We'll get Claire too."

110

"Okay," Becky said. "We'll find her. She couldn't have gotten far."

"I don't know," Honey said. "That girl is pretty fast."

Honey and Becky took off running.

"Let's try the school yard," Becky said. "She .might be in the playground."

"Okay," Honey said.

But Darcy wasn't anywhere on the school

grounds. They checked the playground. They checked near the giant raven statue, and they checked behind every building and even the parking lot. But no Darcy.

Honey stood near the raven statue. She knew it wasn't her fault that Darcy flubbed the trick. But she also thought that maybe, just maybe, if she had been nicer Darcy would have headed straight for her instead of just hiding out somewhere.

111

"How about the Green?" Honey said. "There's plenty of hiding places there."

"Good idea," Becky said.

They checked around the Headless Horseman statue. They checked near the clock tower. Becky even went inside the clock tower, but Darcy wasn't there either.

"Come on," Honey said. "Let's go find Claire. She's probably at the ball field."

The friends ran as hard as they could.

Honey's backpack bounced on her back.

"Where on earth could she be?" Becky said.

Claire was easy to find. She was hitting fly balls with Noah on the field. Honey ran out to the batter's box. "Come on, Claire. Darcy is missing. You have to help find her."

"What do you mean missing?"

Honey told Claire the whole story as quickly as she could without leaving out too many of the details.

"Gee," Claire said. "Your brother is a better magician than I thought."

"It's not magic," Honey said. "She just ran away."

"Maybe someone should tell her parents or Officer Ortiz," Noah said.

"Good idea," Honey said. "You go tell her folks. We'll search the town."

Honey, Becky, and Claire searched and searched. This was getting serious. Honey felt a little relief when she saw Officer Ortiz driving slowly down the road. She shrugged when he saw her.

"Don't worry, we'll find her," Officer Ortiz called.

They searched until they felt exhausted. Honey checked her cell for the gazillionth time hoping Darcy had called or texted or that maybe Harry texted because he had found her. But no. No texts. No calls. "Come on," Honey said. "Let's go back to my house and talk with my parents."

113

"Good idea," Becky said.

Honey felt tired. Not just because she was running so much but also because she was worried. It seemed like they had been searching for hours and hours, but it wasn't really all that long.

"No one is ever truly lost," Turtle said. "Just

keep looking. Sometimes in the most unlikely places."

Honey stopped walking. She gave herself a face palm as usual. "I know exactly where she is."

"What?" Claire asked. "Where?"

"She's at my house."

"Your house?" Becky exclaimed. "Why would she go to your house?"

"Maybe she was looking for me. Where else would she go?"

"Okay," Claire said. "Let's go check it out."

Honey took off running again. She ran straight around to the back of her house, but she didn't see Darcy.

"Rats! Double rats!" Honey said. "I was really hoping she'd be here. Sitting right in the gazebo, waiting for me."

"Now what?" Becky said.

Honey walked closer to the gazebo. "Shhhhhh," she whispered. "Do you hear that?"

Becky said, "It sounds like a puppy or something."

"Nope, it's crying. And it's coming from over there. Behind the garage."

The girls crept closer.

115

"Darcy!" Honey said. "We found you."

Darcy looked up. Tears streamed down her cheeks. She swiped some away.

"I can't do anything right," Darcy said. "Not one single thing. I messed up Harry's show. I messed up art club. I can't sing..." she sniffed.

Honey sat on the grass next to her. "It's okay. Harry's show was fine. He's not mad or anything. He's just worried."

Darcy sobbed louder. "I didn't want to make anyone worry."

"Then you shouldn't have run away," Becky said.

"I'm sorry," Darcy said.

Honey put her arm around Darcy's shoulders. "I don't get it."

"Get what?" Darcy blubbered.

"Nothing ever rattles you. You keep bouncing back. This is different. Even after I said that mean thing, you didn't cry or run away."

Darcy sobbed even harder. "I just wanted to make friends."

Honey sat there. She didn't really know what to say. She only knew that Darcy Diamond was probably not the Princess of Annoying. She was just a girl who wanted to fit into Sleepy Hollow.

117

"Jumpin' tiddlywinks," Honey said. "Look, I should let Harry know you're okay. And he can get a hold of Officer Ortiz and your parents."

"Officer?" Darcy said.

"Well, yeah. We had to tell him. We searched and searched and couldn't find you."

"But I was right here."

"Yeah," Honey said. "I finally figured it out."

Honey texted Harry. He texted back. "grt. will call off hounds."

"But I still don't understand." Honey tucked her phone into her back pocket. She offered Darcy a hand so she could stand.

"If not being able to sing or draw does make you sad, why do you pretend it doesn't?"

118

"I keep trying and trying and then I pretend I don't care because it's easier that way. I don't like feeling sad."

"Well, that's a relief," Honey said. "I was thinking you were some kind of superwoman. You know, nerves of steel and all that."

Darcy shook her head. "No. I just don't want anyone to know I...I stink at everything!" she blurted.

Becky gave a small chuckle. "That's impossible. Nobody can stink at everything."
"Yeah," Claire said. "Ever try baseball?"

Darcy laughed. "I couldn't throw a ball three feet and every time I swing a bat I fall down."

Honey took a deep breath. "Come on. Let's go inside. We'll figure this out. I bet we'll find something you're good at."

"Are you sure?" Darcy asked. "I don't want to be a bother."

Honey laughed. "So now you don't want to be a bother. Sheesh. Come on inside."

Darcy stopped walking. "How come you want to help me now—for real I mean? After... after what you said."

"Because I do," Honey said. "Friends help each other no matter what." Honey had to catch her breath. She could hardly believe she had just said those words. But then again, how do any friendships begin? Friendships just had a way of happening. It was that way for her and Becky. Honey couldn't even remember how they became friends. Claire was a little bit of a different story. They had always known each other, been in the same classes, went to the same church, and were partners in the three-legged race at the Sleepy Hollow Halloween Party, but actually becoming friends took a little work. Honey smiled at Darcy. "Yeah, it's what friends do."

"Even if one of those friends talks too much?" Darcy said.

Honey laughed. "I said I was sorry about that."

They started toward the house when Honey snapped her fingers. "That's it!" she said. "I got it! I know just where Darcy will fit in."

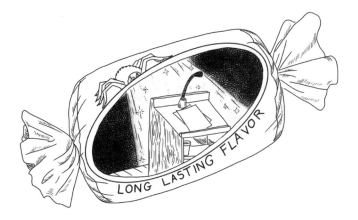

THE GREAT IDEA

H oney ran on ahead into the kitchen. She couldn't be more excited if she tried. Finding Darcy was great, but what Honey had up her sleeve this time was dynamite. She had the perfect plan. There was no way Darcy could mess this one up.

Honey threw open the back door and out bounded Half Moon. He was barking to beat the band. "Settle down, Half," Honey said. "We got work to do."

Becky, Claire, and Darcy quickly followed behind.

"What are you doing?" Becky called.

"You'll see. Everyone come into the kitchen."

The first thing Honey did was snag a bag of cookies.

"Whoa, whoa, Honey," Mom said. "What's going on?"

"Didn't you hear, Mom?"

Becky, Claire, and Darcy stood in a line.

"What on Earth?" Mom said.

Honey took a bite of chocolate chip cookie. "We lost Darcy for a while. But it's good now. We found her." Honey looked at Darcy and smiled. "It was destiny."

Darcy smiled back. "Destiny."

That was when Harry appeared. "Darcy," he said. "What happened?"

The kitchen was getting crowded, and Mom almost blew her stack. "Okay, someone better tell me what is going on."

"I will," Honey said.

"Fine," Mom said. "Now spill it. But first, everyone find a seat."

"Okay, so here's what happened." Honey proceeded to tell her mom the whole story. Even the part about buying her new top. "And now, here we are, and I, the one and only Honey Moon, girl genius, have figured out Darcy Diamond's destiny. Well, besides us being friends."

"Wow," Darcy said. "You mean that? We're really friends?"

Becky shot Honey a look since Becky was already Honey's best friend.

"Yeah, yeah," Honey said. "We're friends. But what I have in mind is something so wonderful, so earth-shattering it could mean your entire future. I mean this is not just about fitting in at school. It's about...about fitting into the whole world."

Darcy's eyes grew wide. "Oh my gosh, I'm so excited. Tell me, Honey. Tell me now. I hope it's really good. I hope it's fun. I think destinies should be fun. Don't you?"

"It's the best," Honey said.

"Okay, so, we all know Darcy loves to talk, right?"

"Honey!" Mom said. "That's not kind."

"It's all right, Mrs. Moon," Darcy said. "I do talk a lot. I love to talk. I can talk about practically anything for a really long time. My mother says I'm like a machine. My dad says I have diarrhea of the mouth."

Claire burst into laughter. "Now that's funny."

Honey, Becky, Claire, and even Harry had about had it. They couldn't contain it any longer, and they all burst out laughing. Honey's mom tried to contain them, but even she couldn't help it and started to laugh. Which of course, made Darcy laugh, and then Half Moon got in on the deal and barked like mad.

So it was only natural when Honey's dad and little brother walked in that they just stood there with their mouths open. That is until Dad said, "What in the world?"

"Oh, Dad," Honey said. But she was still giggling. "Hi."

Mom was laughing so hard she could hardly catch her breath. "John," she said. "You're home."

But the thing about laughing, that Honey knew very well, is that it's contagious. All of a sudden, Harvest started to giggle, then Dad joined in, and Half Moon barked even louder. Honey thought it was one of the funniest things to happen in the Moon house for quite some time.

"What is so funny?" Dad asked.

"I am," Darcy said. "I'm what's so funny because I talk so much. I'm like a machine you can't turn off."

"Diarrhea of the mouth," Claire said.

Dad shook his head. "Okay, okay. I guess I get it."

Then the laughter died down, and everyone grew quiet. Honey felt everyone's eyes on her. She was the one with the plan that would somehow put Darcy Diamond's penchant for talking to good use.

"Well," Darcy said. "Tell me, Honey. What is your plan?"

"Okay, okay, listen up," Honey said. "I was at the bookstore today, and I saw a poster."

"A poster?" Darcy asked.

Honey told Darcy and everyone else about the public speaking class and contest.

"Wow," Darcy said. "You mean I'll get to talk, and no one will tell me to stop?"

Claire laughed again.

"Sort of," Honey's dad said. "The class will teach you things like poise and presence and how to make a public address—using humor and stories and other public speaking techniques. But most speeches do have a time limit."

"I don't know, Dad," Harry said. "Some of Reverend McAdams' sermons go on forever!"

That started the laughing again but not for quite as long as before.

"Anyway," Honey said. "I think it's the perfect thing for you, Darcy."

"Yeah," Darcy said. "I...I guess so. But what about school?" She looked at her feet and a giant pout formed on her face.

Honey sighed. She sat at the kitchen table. "Now what? Darcy?"

"The public speaking is at the church. What can I do at school?"

Honey and Darcy exchanged worried looks.

"Just stop trying so hard," Honey said. "Just be a regular kid, and you'll fit in."

"That's good advice," Mom said. "You'll find your way. Everyone does. The important thing is that you don't give up."

"Thank you, Mrs. Moon. That's what my mom keeps telling me, too."

"She's a wise woman," Mom said.

Now that the excitement had died down and Darcy was safe and sound, Honey, Becky,

Claire, and this time, Darcy decided to spend the rest of their Saturday together. Of course, Darcy found it difficult not to chatter on and on and on about the public speaking contest. She was already trying to come up with a subject.

Honey tried to change the subject, but it didn't work until Claire suggested everyone go to the park and play some ball. At first, Darcy

said no, but then she changed her mind—now that everyone knew she stunk at baseball.

And she was not kidding.

Claire stood on the pitcher's mound. Darcy stood at home plate with the bat over her shoulder. Except she had no stance and no form. Noah, who was already at the park, tried to show her how to hold the bat and how to stand in the batter's box. He even stood behind her with his arms around her to show how it was done. But that made the girls laugh and make kissy noises.

"Aww, cut it out," Noah said. "I was just showing her how to stand."

"We know, Noah," Honey said. "We're sorry." But then she made more kissy noises when he wasn't looking.

But even with Noah's instruction, every time Darcy swung the bat it was always too late—the ball had already passed home plate—and she fell on the ground.

"Another case of trying too hard," Honey said.

"But at least this time she isn't running away or pretending it doesn't bother her," Becky said.

Nope. Darcy laughed at herself. She stood tall at the plate. So what if she couldn't swing. Big deal. She could talk.

132

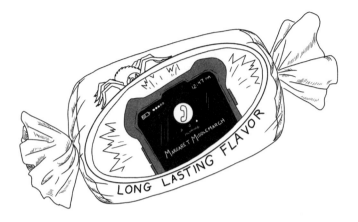

YOU'RE A TURTLE

Honey was feeling pretty good about herself and about Darcy Diamond that evening. She was feeling so good that when Mom asked her to do an extra chore—fold towels and put them in the linen closet—she did it with a smile.

"Sure, Mom," she said. "Glad to."

Honey sat in the living room with the basket of towels. She was watching a Sleepy Hollow original show—*Three Mummies and a Vampire*. It was pretty funny. She especially liked the bumbling vampire, Vince.

Mom peeked her head in after she had put Harvest down for the night. "Doing okay?" she asked.

"Sure, Mom. I'll have these towels folded in no time flat."

"I know you will." Then Mom stepped all the way into the living room. "I'm proud of you, for watching after Darcy and for coming up with that amazing idea."

"Thanks, Mom. You know, it feels good to do the right thing."

"It sure does, Honey Moon. It sure does."

Honey placed a folded towel into the clothes basket. "I think Darcy Diamond really was my destiny. I mean it was my destiny to help her."

"Sure," Mom said. "But Honey, destiny is a pretty big thing."

"I know. But it's like I always say, 'I go where I am needed.' This time it came to me."

Mom hung back a few moments and watched Honey. Sometimes moms did these things just because they liked to. And Honey understood this.

"Oh," Mom said after a while. "I meant to ask you how your shopping trip went. Did you get your blouse?"

"Yes, I did." But that reminded her of what Becky said—about needing a training bra. She cringed a little.

"Hey, Mom, so...I was meaning to ask you about something." Honey set another folded towel onto the stack on the coffee table.

"You might want to start another stack or dump the towels on the couch and put the folded ones in the basket—just a suggestion."

Honey rolled her eyes. Moms had a tendency to stare, and kids had a tendency to roll their eyes. It was just the way of the world.

"I'm sorry," Mom said. "What did you want to ask me?"

Honey looked around. The last thing she needed was for Harry to walk in right now. What she had to say was delicate. Not for Harry's ears.

"Sooo," Honey said. "When I was trying the blouse on...well, Becky was there and she..." Honey had to take another breath.

"She what?"

"She said it made me look like I...like I needed a training bra." She said the last part of the sentence really fast. Sometimes difficult things were better blurted out all at once.

"Ohhhh, I see," Mom said. "Well, now that you mention it, we could get you one. See how it makes you feel."

"Will it feel tight and scrunchy?"

"Nope. Not if it fits well. It might make you feel pretty. We can get one with lace."

"Oooooo, okay. Can I get a pink one? Or will it be orange and black and have stupid spiders all over it?"

Mom laughed. "No. We can find a pink one."

Honey took another breath and let it out so hard that the stack of towels crashed to the floor. "I think I'll try it your way, Mom."

Mom stood. She kissed Honey's head and said, "Good idea. We'll go shopping early next week."

"Thanks, Mom."

Honey smiled so wide she thought her face might crack. This had turned out to be a very good day. Nothing could possibly go wrong now.

After church the next day, Honey was

back to work folding laundry. And she was still feeling pretty good. She had almost made it through the entire weekend without any trouble. Her mother's cell buzzed. Honey looked around. She spotted her bag. "Mom," Honey called. "You cell is buzzing."

Mom called from the kitchen, "See who it is, please."

Honey dug deep into mother's bag and found the phone. "It's Mrs. Middlemarch."

"Uhm," Mom said walking into the living room. "What could she want?"

"Probably something to do with Harry."

Mom clicked the phone. "Hello, Margaret. How are you?"

Honey watched her mom. She couldn't hear what Mrs. Middlemarch was saying but when her Mom said, "I think that's a marvelous idea. Honey will be so glad you called," Honey was surprised.

"What will I be glad about?" Honey asked.

"That was Mrs. Middlemarch," Mom said.

"I know. I was the one who told you."

"Oh, yeah." Mom sat on the easy chair. "She told me about the public speaking club. The Sleepy Hollow Young Speakers."

"Yeah," Honey said. "I was also the one to tell you."

139

"Right, well, she wants you to join. She thinks you'd make a great asset to the club, and she wants you to participate in the contest."

Honey felt her eyes grow big. "Me? In the very same contest as Darcy? But, Mom..."

"I know, Honey," Mom said. "But this could be a great opportunity and stuff like this always looks good on college applications."

Honey folded the last towel and set it in

the basket. "I don't know. Can I think about it?"

"Sure. But don't take long. The first meeting is Wednesday."

Honey picked up the clothes basket. "I'll take these upstairs, and then I'm going to bed."

"Okay, good night, dear."

"Good night, Mom."

After she had loaded the linen closet with fresh towels, Honey went to her room. She closed the door and flopped belly first on her bed. "Arrggghhhhh. Jumpin' tiddlywinks! I don't want to go up against Darcy."

"Why?"

Honey lifted her head. She saw Turtle hanging on her desk chair. His googly eyes were looking straight at her. "Why?" he asked again.

"Because it's not fair. I don't want her to

lose. The whole reason was to find something she could do."

"But Honey, if, and I say if, she loses that doesn't mean she failed. Not as long as she gives her best effort. And by the way, what makes you so sure you will win?"

Honey sat straight up. "Because I'm good

at all my reports and stuff at school, and well, I'm just good at speeches."

"Hum dee dum dum," Turtle said. "We shall see."

Honey changed into her nightgown, the one with the little turtles on it. "I'll talk to Darcy tomorrow."

When morning came, Honey was awakened by a loud crash of thunder and lightning. "Rain, just great," Honey said.

"I rather enjoy the rain," Turtle said.

"You're a turtle, that's why."

Honey grabbed her bag after dressing for the day and digging her rain jacket out from the pile on her closet floor.

Mrs. Wilcox, Harvest's babysitter, was in the kitchen trying to get Harvest to eat scrambled eggs.

"Good morning, Honey," Mrs. Wilcox said.

"Morning," Honey said. "How are you?"

"I'm fine, dear. Your mother had an early shift. There's scrambled eggs and bacon."

"Yum," Honey said. One of the best things about Mrs. Wilcox was that she did not make smoothies for breakfast. Honey took four pieces of bacon and a bunch of eggs. She sat at the table and was quickly joined by Harry who snagged the remaining bacon and eggs.

"Oh boy," he said, "love it when Mom goes in early."

Honey chewed her bacon, but she was also chewing on something else. What to do about the Speakers Club?

"I will be late after school," Harry said. "I'm meeting the guys for pizza."

"Fine," Mrs. Wilcox said.

Harry grabbed his bag and bolted out the

front door.

Honey finished her breakfast and headed out the door.

"Oh, Honey," Mrs. Wilcox called. "I saw the notice about the Young Speakers Club at the bookstore. I think you would be great for that."

Honey smiled. "Thank you, Mrs. Wilcox. Maybe."

The rain was falling harder now. Honey pulled her hood over her head just as another crash of thunder clanged overhead. She ran, jumping over some puddles and stomping in others.

As usual, she met up with Becky and Claire at the Green. Darcy was there also, and Honey didn't mind so much. Except she did feel a little nervous. She didn't know if she should tell her that she would be joining the Young Speakers Club or not.

She decided not to. Not yet, anyway.

School was pretty ordinary until lunchtime recess. That was when the cat was let out of the bag. And it wasn't Honey. Nope, it was good old Claire Kligore.

Honey, Becky, Claire, and Darcy had managed to get the swings. This was something that did not happen often. Honey had been trying for two years to get the school to put in more swings. But they wouldn't— budget restrictions. Or more likely Mayor Kligore restrictions.

Anyway, Clarice was hanging near the swings. Honey thought she was looking particularly smug.

"She's up to something," Honey said.

"Yeah, she is," Claire said. "I wonder what."

"How do you know?" Darcy asked. "She's just standing there. I mean it's okay to just stand isn't it?"

"Not for Clarice Kligore," Honey said.

Honey leaped off the swing. "Hey, Clarice," she said. "What gives?"

"Nothing much, Moon," Clarice said.

Becky, Claire, and Darcy formed a semi-circle around Honey.

"Soooo," Clarice said. "My dad tells me you are joining the Young Speakers."

Honey felt her eyebrows wrinkle. "What? How would he know?"

"Simple, doofus," Clarice said. "My dad runs the paper, and Mrs. Middlemarch works for him. They were discussing the contest, and that's when she told him because he had said he didn't want any Moons in the club."

"No, he didn't," Becky said. "He can't keep Honey from joining."

"Maybe not," Clarice said. "But he can keep a Moon from winning."

Honey caught Darcy's eye. She looked a little scared.

"You can tell your father that a Moon is joining the club and that a Moon will win the contest."

"Suit yourself," Clarice said. "But don't say

you weren't warned."

Clarice walked off across the playground.

Honey knew she was going to have to talk to Darcy. But she said a quick prayer that the whistle would blow and she could avoid it—at least until after school.

"I don't understand," Darcy said. "Are you in the club? That's fine with me. I don't mind my best friend being in the same club. And I don't even mind if we both enter the contest. And I don't mind if you win. But you know what they say, may the best woman win."

The whistle blew. Honey had no time to say anything. The students took off toward school. Honey was in a pickle—again. She didn't want Clarice's bullying to stop her from winning, but she also wanted Darcy to win. This was one king-sized dilemma. The trouble was, she had play practice right after school. Talking to Darcy would have to wait.

Honey and Becky headed into the

café-gym-atorium for practice. Mrs. Fortissimo was already there getting the stage set up with the help of a couple boys.

"I practiced my lines," Becky said. "I can't believe I get to play Glinda."

"I practiced, too," Honey said. "I love being Dorothy."

Mrs. Tenure arrived and got the entire cast situated for rehearsal. "Today," she said, "we'll just be running our lines, and those of you with singing parts will practice your songs."

"Okay," Honey said. "I love singing 'Over the Rainbow.'"

Practice went off without a hitch pretty much. Scarlet Lincoln, who was playing Auntie Em, said she might throw up, but she didn't. And Clarice, who was now, all of a sudden, playing the wicked witch, did her part effortlessly. Although, every chance she got, she gave Honey another warning about the contest.

Honey did well, and so did Becky. But Honey was more pleased that practice was over. She had to find Darcy and talk to her about the Young Speakers.

"Come on," Honey said, grabbing Becky's hand. "Let's go find Darcy."

"I can't," Becky said. "I have to go straight home today."

"Rats," Honey said. "Okay, well I'll try and find her."

Fortunately, Honey did not have to really hunt for Darcy at all. She was waiting in the school playground.

"Hey," Darcy called. "I was waiting for you. I thought that was a good idea. To wait. That way we can walk home together. How was play practice? I bet you did a great job."

"Darcy!" Honey said. "Slow down."

"Sorry," Darcy said.

"Look, I don't know any better way to say this. I'm joining Young Speakers, and I'm going to enter the contest."

Darcy looked at Honey with squinty eyes. "Really? Great. Like I said. It will be good to be in a club with my best friend. And who says you are going to win the contest? Even you said I'm a great talker. I'm sure to win."

Honey took a step back. "Now hold on. Being a good talker doesn't make you a great speaker. There is a difference."

Darcy shrugged. "So what? I'm still gonna win."

Then Darcy took off running across the school yard.

Honey gave herself another face palm. "Jumpin' tiddlywinks!" The trouble was, Honey didn't know if Darcy was really that positive or if she was just covering up again. "Time will tell," Honey said. "May the best girl win!" She shrugged off her turtle backpack and looked into his googly eyes. "And it's going to be me!"

"Now who's being a little too sure of herself or maybe just covering up?"

"Me? Nah. I got this. You'll see. I'm going to give the best speech ever!"

"Hum, hum, hum."

152

THE YOUNG
SPEAKERS CLUB

The first meeting of the Sleepy Hollow Young Speakers Club was all set to start. Honey had arrived at the Old North Church a few minutes early—she liked to scope out her competition and get the best seat. Mrs. Middlemarch was already there, of course, setting things up. She had a white board with multi-colored dry erase markers and a podium. That was all.

"I guess speakers don't need much else," Honey said.

"For now, Honey, this is all you need. And a good story or a good speech," Mrs. Middlemarch said. Then she grabbed a box from a table. "Honey, will you place one of these notebooks and a pen on every seat. I'm expecting six young speakers."

"Six? Is that all?"

154

"Oh, I think that's a fine number. I'm glad your new friend Darcy Diamond is joining us."

Honey set a notebook on a chair. "Me, too. She really needed to find a club or something. I think she'll be a great young speaker but..." Honey stopped talking. She was going to say, "But I'm the best." She didn't. And that was a good thing because Darcy had just entered the room.

"Hello," Darcy said with a smile as large as the Grand Canyon. "My name is Darcy Diamond. I'm here for the Young Speakers Club. I can't wait to learn how to be a good public speaker. Did you know that people are more afraid of public speaking than they are of dying? Imagine that!"

Mrs. Middlemarch gave a slight chuckle. Honey lifted her eyebrows and said, "What did I tell you? She loves to talk."

Mrs. Middlemarch ignored Honey. "Well, I'm so glad you came, Darcy. But I suggest you remove that huge wad of bubble gum before you speak."

"Oh, sure, no problem," Darcy said.

The other kids arrived. Honey recognized all of them from school or from around the town. She was most surprised to see Clarice Kligore arrive.

"What is she doing here?" Honey whispered to Darcy.

"Don't know. Guess she wants to speak."

Mrs. Middlemarch wasted no time getting the meeting started. She asked everyone to go around and state their name and why they joined the club. Honey was particularly interested in what Clarice would say.

"Yeah," Clarice said, "name's Clarice Kligore. I'm the mayor's daughter." Then she paused and made eye contact with everyone in the group. It felt more like a threat than a greeting. "I'm here on account of my father—the mayor—thinks it'll be good for when I become an executive in his biz."

"Oh," Mrs. Middlemarch said. "That's just fine, Clarice. Just fine."

The meeting went on for about an hour. Mrs. Middlemarch talked about a lot of things, and then she mentioned the contest.

"The topic, or your thesis, is laughter."

That made everyone laugh. Except for Clarice who said, "That's stupid."

But Mrs. Middlemarch was undaunted. "Then tell us why laughter is stupid—in your speech."

Clarice didn't say a word. She just folded her arms across her chest and scowled like an angry dog.

After Mrs. Middlemarch had dismissed the group, Darcy wasted no time in telling Honey how excited she was to be part of the group.

"And I just can't wait to write my speech. I love to laugh. Don't you? Laughter is a great thing. It just makes everyone feel good, and it's just...oh, so contagious, not in a bad way—"

"Darcy!" Honey exclaimed. "Save it for your speech. Write it down."

"Yeah, Motor Mouth," Clarice Kligore called from across the room. "It's not like you're gonna win but really, do you ever shut up?"

"Don't listen to Old Spooky Jaws," Honey said. "Come on, we can walk home together."

"Great," Darcy said. "Let's go. But I wish Clarice was nicer. Why is she so mean? Do you know why she is so mean?"

Honey pulled open the church door and let Darcy through. "She just is. Born that way, I suppose."

"Well, if anyone needed to laugh more, I'd say it was Clarice. And not evil laughs like she does. Good laughs, like you and me."

158

"Right," Honey said. "Remember to save it for your speech. We have two weeks to write it."

"Plenty of time," Darcy said. "Plenty of time."

Honey was busy watching a game show on TV when Harry walked into the living room. "Hey," he said. "Shouldn't you be working on your speech?"

"Nope," Honey said, "I'm not worried. I got it all under control. As usual."

"Two weeks is not a lot of time, and you've

already blown one week."

Honey looked away from her show. "What? Really?"

"Yeah, remember? You went to the meeting last night. That makes one week."

"Oh," Honey said. "So I better get a jump on...THIS!"

Just as she said the words she pulled some pages from behind the couch pillow. "Ah ha! I already finished my glorious, most wonderful speech that is going to catapult me into the limelight."

Harry laughed. "You got me."

"See that. I'm making people laugh already."

160

Harry grabbed the pages from her. "I think the point is to talk about laughter, not tell jokes and make people laugh."

"I can do both. You'll see."

Harry glanced through the pages and then gave them back. "I'm not going to that. Sit through six boring speeches? No way!"

Honey pouted. She whined a little. "Awwww, my big brother isn't coming?"

Harry shook his head. "Nope. And you can't make me."

"But I can!"

Harry spun around and saw their dad standing there with his arms crossed across his chest.

"Oh, hey, Dad," Harry said. "I didn't know you were there."

"Obviously, Harry," Dad said. "And yes, you will go to the speech reading contest day or whatever they call it."

Honey laughed.

"But Dad," Harry said. "I don't want to."

Honey sashayed past Harry toward the steps. "But you have to, brother."

"Don't be sassy, Honey," Dad said.

Honey sat at her desk and fired up her laptop. "Might need a few polishing touches," she said as she pulled up her speech.

"Laughter is the best medicine," she read.

"It sure can be," Turtle said. "It can also be the worst kind of derision."

"Derision. You mean like when someone laughs at another person when they make a mistake or fall down or do something totally nerdy like Harry."

"Yes, it's all part of it. Right?"

Honey read her speech.

"I suppose I could mention some of that kind of stuff. Darcy probably is, and I bet that Clarice Kligore is writing something totally mean-spirited. Ugh."

Honey worked on her speech a while longer—until she could barely keep her eyes open and focused. After one final read through she leaned back in her chair feeling quite pleased with her work. "Another A+ for me."

But as she got changed into her nightgown and climbed into bed she couldn't help but wonder if maybe, just maybe, Darcy Diamond had the chops to win. If only she could get her hands on Darcy's speech.

MAY THE BEST GIRL WIN

Honey hurried to school early the next morning. She wanted to meet up with Becky and Claire before Darcy—if that was even possible. She had texted them: mt me erly.

She saw Becky first, and then Claire walking a little like a zombie. "This better be good," Claire called. "I still had ten minutes to sleep."

They met under the shadow of the Headless Horseman which seemed even more sinister than usual this morning. Honey glared at it. "Boo!" she said, trying to fend off any bad vibes.

"Yeah," Becky said. "What gives, Honey?"

"Okay, so you guys know I joined the Young Speakers Club right?"

"Of course," Claire said. "Everybody knows."

"Well, I wrote my speech about laughter, but I'm worried about Darcy." She took a quick look around to make sure Darcy had not shown up. She did not want Darcy to overhear this time.

"Why?" Claire said. "You're a great writer. And speaker. You'll win hands down!"

"Maybe," Honey said. "But I want to be sure. Sooooo, and this is where you two come in, I want you to help me get a look at her speech."

Becky gasped. "Honey Moon! That's terrible. No, I will not help."

Honey looked at Claire. But even Claire was a little undecided and usually Claire was up for pretty much any caper. "Wow," Claire said. "I don't know. It's like cheating."

"Yeah," Becky said. "And I thought you wanted to help Darcy."

"I do, but...but then this contest thing came up, and Clarice Kligore said her dad didn't want me to do it and Mrs. Middlemarch is all proud of me and—"

165

"And now Darcy Diamond doesn't matter anymore," Becky said.

Honey looked away. She did not like the feelings that had bubbled up inside her stomach. Becky was right. This was kind of beside the point and well, not kind.

"But what if she wins?"

"Then she wins. And if you win it will be fair and square. Not because you cheated."

"Okay, okay I get ya."

Yeah, Becky was right. Why would Honey want to win a contest she cheated in? That would make the whole thing meaningless.

The girls walked on toward school. "See ya, Horseface!" Honey called to the statue.

"I'll tell you whose speech I want to hear," Becky said.

"Whose?" Honey asked.

"Clarice Kligore's."

"Yeah, it's probably all about how much all the spooky junk around town is supposed to make us happy and laugh," Claire said.

"Yeah, like we're supposed to laugh when a skeleton jumps out of the mailbox. Like that's funny," Becky said.

"Or maybe she'll speak about how funny coffins and bats and cemeteries can be," Becky said. "Ugh, no way, is she gonna win!"

They walked a little further before Darcy caught up with them. "Hey," she called. "Wait up!"

"Hey," Honey said.

"Hey," Darcy said. "I'm glad I caught up with you guys. I thought I was late, but I think you were early. How come you were so early?"

Honey shrugged. "Just because."

Darcy shrugged. "Okay."

But Honey couldn't help but feel a little twinge of guilt. She had planned to torpedo Darcy's speech. She kind of wanted to confess, but she knew that would only make her feel better, not Darcy. As they walked, Honey's backpack began to feel a little heavier with each step. She thought about the lies she had told earlier, lies that helped her escape Darcy.

"Okay, okay," Honey said. "I know. It wasn't cool."

"What?" Claire asked. "What wasn't cool?"

"Oh, nothing," Honey said. "I was just thinking out loud. Anyway, tell us about your speech, Darcy. If you want to."

Darcy smiled. "Sure, but just a little. I don't want to give it all away."

Ugh. Honey shook her head.

Darcy did tell the girls a little about her speech, but she didn't say much, which for Darcy was really something. But what she did say struck a little terror into Honey's heart.

"My theme is laughter is the best medicine."

"Jumpin' tiddlywinks!" Honey gave herself another face palm. She whispered to Turtle, "We might as well wear the exact same outfits, too."

The next few days went by quickly. Honey practiced her speech every day after play practice. She also continued to tweak and polish the words. She even listened to some famous orators on YouTube and tried to emulate them. Speakers like Sojourner Truth, Martin Luther King, Jr., and Eleanor Roosevelt. She practiced using her hands and smiling and making a connection with the audience—all the stuff Mrs. Middlemarch had taught them.

The day of the contest arrived. Honey woke early, even though she didn't want to. She wanted to get more rest, but her brain woke her up with the words of her speech turning like socks in the dryer.

After getting dressed for school, she chose what she would wear at the speech—her new blouse and a purple and white striped skirt. She rummaged through her closet and found her black flats. They were the most comfortable, well next to her sneakers, so the flats were best.

She held the blouse up in the mirror. "I'm

not only going to be the best speaker but also the best-dressed." Then she sailed off in a daydream and imagined herself walking the red carpet, waving to adoring fans on her way to accept her award. "Thank you, thank you," she said. "I couldn't do it without all of you—the little people." But then she shook her head. Sojourner Truth would never say such a thing nor would MLK or Mrs. Middlemarch. Honey had grown to really like and appreciate Mrs. M. She had a way of teaching that made even really hard concepts easy to understand. And Honey thought she was a pretty awesome speaker.

She was just about to return from her dream when the door burst open. It was Harry.

"Caught ya," he said.

"Doing what, numskull?"

"Practicing for the big speech like you're about to win an Academy Award."

Honey hung her blouse in the closet. "So what? It's good to dream. And it's good to practice."

"Yeah, yeah, I know. I practice my magic tricks a hundred times. But you know, it is possible to practice too much."

"That's what Dad told me last night. But I just want to be ultra-prepared—like I am for everything."

Harry walked into the room. He looked at the speech on the laptop screen. "Why's this so important? I thought you were helping Darcy."

"I am helping Darcy, and it wasn't important until that lame-brained, bully, Clarice Kligore, told me her father didn't want me in it and that she, of all people, was going to win."

Harry's eyes grew wide. "Kligore. What's it to him who wins some amateur speech contest?"

Honey closed her laptop and stuffed it

into her backpack. "Oh, don't get all riled and sweaty, brother, he's probably just afraid I'll talk about why Sleepy Hollow is such a laughable place or something. You know, tell people not to take it so seriously."

Harry looked out the window. "Yeah, that could be it. But just be careful. And I think I will go, just in case."

Honey sighed. "Fine. Come to the speeches. Just don't do anything. Maybe leave your magic wand behind."

"We'll see."

Honey took her time walking to the Town Green to meet up with Becky, Claire, and probably Darcy. There was a light mist falling, and the usual Sleepy Hollow aromas—pumpkin spice, sage, and cinnamon—made her smile. She enjoyed the gray sky and cool breeze. Even though it wasn't a day that most people would consider spectacular, at least not weather wise, Honey Moon felt fine. She passed Mrs. Spiderwick's house and counted six new plastic spiders on her lawn. She laughed. "Now see, you stupid spiders, I'm laughing. Laughter is the best medicine to chase away fear." But at the same time, Honey was not naïve, she also knew that sometimes laughing at fear was kind of a ruse—just something you did to make it all seem okay. She had written that in her speech.

She hiked her backpack high on her shoulders. "You've worked hard," Turtle said.

173

"Thanks. Life takes hard work. Determination —that's a good word isn't it?"

"Yep. Just remember to stay the course."

"I will," she whispered. She had just spotted Becky near the statue.

Honey waved. "Good morning."

"Morning," Becky called.

Then Claire popped out from behind an oak. And then Darcy.

"Today's the day," Honey said. "The big speeches."

The girls walked on toward school.

"I'm so excited. I mean like never before," Darcy said. "I've been practicing and practicing. And I could barely sleep last night. How about you, Honey. Have you been practicing? Could you sleep?"

"Yeah," Honey said. "Maybe even over-practicing."

"Over-practicing?" Claire asked. "That's not possible."

"Sure it is," Becky said. "Sometimes you get so familiar with something that it loses its excitement and gets boring, or you get so sure of yourself you make mistakes."

Claire stopped. She twisted her mouth up. "Uhm," she said. "Yeah. Like in baseball. It's better to go to the plate with confidence but not too much confidence."

175

"Right," Darcy said. "Mrs. Middlemarch said a few nerves are perfectly normal and A-OK."

The mist had turned to a more constant rain, so the girls picked up their pace. "I hope this day goes quickly," Honey said. "It's going to be torture to wait."

"Yeah, me too," Darcy said. "I'm gonna be watching the clock all day. And you know that watching the clock just makes it go slower. I mean, why do we do that?"

Honey, Becky, and Claire shook their heads.

"Come on," Claire said. "Let's run. The rain is really coming down now."

Darcy was correct. Watching the clock only made the day go slow. But Honey couldn't help it. She saw every tick of every clock. She had trouble paying attention in class. She even let out a few groans and sighs. Mrs. Tenure had to keep reprimanding her. "Eyes on me, Honey Moon," Mrs. Tenure said about a million times. She also had to say the same thing to Darcy. Some of the other kids even started laughing at them. But that was okay. Honey didn't mind, and neither did Darcy, it seemed.

Finally, Mrs. Tenure said, "I know you girls are excited and nervous about the speeches tonight, but you must pay attention in class."

Then Mrs. Tenure called Jerry, the school custodian. He came and hung a black cloth over the clock. That made the whole class crack up and Honey and Darcy shrink in their seats.

"Now," Mrs. Tenure said, "perhaps we can get back to fractions."

"Sorry, Mrs. Tenure," Honey said.

Lunchtime recess went faster. The rain had stopped so they could have outdoor recess. Clarice Kligore showed up at the swings and hassled Honey and Darcy a bit.

"You are so going down, Moon," Clarice said. "I got the best speech. My father made one of his lackey lawyers help me."

"That's cheating," Darcy said.

"So what?" Clarice said. "Dad's lawyers make speeches all the time in court. They know exactly what to do."

"Ha!" Honey said. "Lawyers are boring. And what do they know about laughter? Your speech is going to be the worst."

Clarice balled her hand into a tight fist.

"I wouldn't do that," Honey said. "You'll get kicked out of the contest."

"Just you wait, Honey Moon. I'm gonna speech the socks off ya!"

Honey and Darcy laughed and laughed as Clarice went back to the monkey bars to hang with her lackeys—Paige and Taylor.

"Geeze," Darcy said. "Why is she so mean?"

Honey pumped higher and higher and then she slowed down to a dead stop. "I think it's on account of her mother. She left when Clarice was two years old or something."

"Ugh," Darcy said. "That stinks! And certainly nothing to laugh about. I guess it would make me mean too, at least a little. I don't like to be mean. It's better to be nice. Don't you think? Maybe we can help Clarice start acting nicer."

Honey jumped from the swing when the whistle blew.

"Come on, Darcy," Honey said. "Save your voice for tonight."

"Right," Darcy said. "But are you scared? Nervous?"

"A little," Honey said. "But I'm mostly okay."

"Yeah, me too," Darcy said.

179

"May the best girl win," Honey said.

180

THE COMPETITION

Honey could hardly eat her dinner. And it was her favorite meal. Mom made meatloaf, mashed potatoes with gravy, and green beans—okay she wasn't crazy about the beans, but everything else was scrumptious.

"What's wrong, Honey?" Mom asked. "You've hardly touched your mashed potatoes."

"My stomach is wobbly," Honey said.

"Nervous about your speech?" Dad asked.

Honey nodded and stabbed her meatloaf.

"I get nervous before every performance," Harry said. "But I get over it. Sometimes I pick one person in the audience and perform for that one person instead of the whole crowd."

Dad chewed and swallowed hard. Then he wagged his fork at Honey. "That's good advice, Snickerdoodle. Just talk to one person you're comfortable with—like me or Mom."

182

Honey sipped iced tea. "It's not that."

"Then what's' causing the bats in the belly?" Mom asked.

"Oh, I don't know. I guess it's Darcy. I really do want her to win. But I want to win also. And that Clarice Kligore ambushed me at recess today and claims her father got one of his lawyers to write her speech."

Dad dropped his fork on his plate. "That's

cheating."

"It sure is," Mom said.

"It's the Kligore way," Harry said.

Honey managed to get a few bites of meatloaf down, and she even swallowed some green beans. Of course, she pinched her nose but still, nutrition is nutrition. Just so she got it down.

183

"Should I throw it? Take a dive?" Honey asked without looking at anyone.

"Absolutely not!" Mom said. "That would be the worst thing you could do."

"Yeah," Harry said. "Don't do that."

Harvest clapped. His mashed potatoes flew off his tray and splattered on the table. But no one seemed to notice or care. That's the way it was with two-year-olds sometimes.

Half Moon licked the potatoes that fell on

the floor. Then he barked as if to say, "No, Honey. Don't do it."

Honey still couldn't eat. She glanced at the kitchen clock. One hour and five minutes to go.

"I know just what will help," Mom said. "Let's get you dressed. There's nothing like getting all dressed up to help a person do well."

"Good, idea," Dad said. "And don't worry, Harry and I will handle the kitchen chores tonight."

184

Harry grunted.

"Thank you," Mom said as she took Honey's hand and led her away from the table. "Save Honey's meal. She will probably be starving when we get home tonight."

"Thanks, Mom. I want to wear my new blouse and my purple and white skirt."

"Sounds nice, dear."

When they reached Honey's bedroom she

said, "And can I wear makeup?"

"Well, how about some lip gloss and a little blush for your cheeks? Nothing heavy."

Honey threw her arms around her Mom. "Thanks, Mom. And can I wear high heels?"

"Uhm, no, I don't think that will be a good idea. You wouldn't want to stumble on your way to the podium. That can happen to even the most grown-up, seasoned public speakers. They mostly wear flats."

"Okay, Mom," Honey said. "I did find my black ballet flats this morning."

"Perfect."

After a quick shower, Honey dressed. She loved her knew lavender top. It was just frilly enough without being too obnoxious. It didn't make her feel like a clown like some flouncy tops did. But when she looked in the mirror her heart sank.

"Mom! Mom! MOM!!" she cried.

Her mother dashed into the room. "Honey, what's wrong?"

"Look at me, that's what's wrong. We never went to the store to buy my...my you know what!"

"Oh Honey, I totally forgot."

186

"Do we have time to go to the BooTique? Please, Mom, I can't go on stage looking like... like this."

"Maybe a tank top for tonight," Mom said.

Honey stamped her foot. "No, I can't. Now, I'll just be more nervous."

Mom looked at Honey's alarm clock. "We have to hurry. We'll stop at the BooTique on the way. But it will be a mad dash for sure."

Honey grabbed her speech. "What about my makeup? Please Mom, I really want make-up."

"Oh, okay, come to my room quickly. And then no time to waste, we'll run out the door."

"You're the best," Honey said.

Mom dabbed Honey's cheeks with a little peach-pink blush. Then she helped Honey use a little pinkish lip gloss.

Honey smiled into her mother's mirror. "I look so pretty."

"Yes, you do," Mom said. "I'll bring the lip gloss because you will want to reapply before you speak."

Honey's stomach went wobbly again. "Oh, yeah. I almost forgot all about the speaking part."

"We better run," Mom said. "To the Batmobile!"

"To the Batmobile," Honey said. She pulled her rain slicker on as she dashed down the steps.

Mom backed down the driveway and onto the street. "We have fifteen minutes, Honey. I hope Sally is still there."

"Oh, she has to be," Honey said. "This is a total disaster if she isn't."

Mom drove as fast as she legally could. She pulled in front of the BooTique. Honey jumped out of the van and ran up to the store door, but a big orange CLOSED sign was hanging in the window.

"Rats!" Honey said. "Closed. Oh, Mom I can't. I can't do the speech. Not now. Not like this."

Mom looked through the window. "I see a light in the back." She knocked. She knocked again. She knocked a third time, and finally, Sally came and unlocked the door.

"Mary," she exclaimed. "Is there a problem?"

"Yes," Honey said. "A huge problem."

"Oh my goodness," Sally said. "What's

happened?"

Mom took Sally aside and spoke quietly to her.

"Oh, I see," Sally said. "I think I have just what you need over here." She led Honey and her mom to a corner in the store. "This is our most popular one."

Honey sighed as she looked at the pretty, pink training bra. There wasn't really much to it, but she knew it would help.

"Come on," Mom said. "You can change in the dressing room."

After a few minor adjustments and after she had put her new, pretty top on, Honey looked in the mirror. She looked so nice and more importantly, she felt so pretty and maybe even just a little bit more grown up.

But there wasn't any time to spare. Her mom grabbed her hand. "Come on, we have to get to the church."

"Good luck," Sally called.

The church was packed. Honey joined the other speakers behind the podium. Honey looked out at the audience. She knew practically everyone there except the woman sitting next to her mother. "Is that your mom?" Honey asked.

"Yeah," Darcy said.

Honey waved. Her mom blew her a kiss, and she was pretty sure she saw Darcy's mother say, "Thank you."

Honey swallowed. She thought that maybe she was the one who should be giving out the thank yous. If it wasn't for Darcy, she might not be sitting there.

"Hi, Honey," Darcy said. "You look so pretty. That top is just perfect."

"Thanks," Honey said. "And you look nice, too."

The other three contestants were boys, so they wore boring suits and ties. Honey looked around. "Where's Clarice?"

"I don't know. The way she was talking you'd think she'd be the first one here."

"Yeah, it's weird. Maybe she chickened out."

"No, such luck," Noah said. "Look." He pointed down the aisle. There was Clarice all decked out in a black suit. She even wore a tie. But she also wore red high heels, and her hair was piled up on her head like a beehive. As she sashayed closer, Honey could see she had been plastered with gobs of make-up.

"She looks like a clown," Darcy whispered.

"She thinks she looks amazing," Honey said. "I'm sure one of her father's employees helped. I bet it was that Cherry Tomato."

"Cherry Tomato?" Darcy said.

"After you've lived here awhile you'll know

who I mean."

Clarice clomped onto the dais. She nearly tripped but recovered in time. Honey had to push a laugh away.

"Hello, losers," Clarice said. "Prepare to be annihilated."

Honey felt a wave of dizziness. "You're the loser."

But fortunately, Mrs. Middlemarch appeared from the side.

"Okay," she said to the group. "Everyone's here. Now remember, speak slowly and clearly, make a connection with your audience, and if you make a mistake don't fret. Just keep going. Remember, it's not a bad idea to laugh at your own mistakes. Not that you will make any. I'm proud of you all."

Honey clapped, and that started all the other speakers clapping. Before she knew it, the whole audience was clapping. Mrs.

Middlemarch smiled and took the podium. She raised her hands, and the crowd settled down.

"There's my dad," Darcy said. "He is so excited; he is videoing the whole thing."

"Nice," Honey said. "He looks like a nerd," she added with a whisper.

"Big time," Darcy said. "Huge, big time nerd. But he makes me laugh."

Mrs. Middlemarch tapped the microphone and then said, "Welcome to the first ever Sleepy Hollow Young Speakers Club Orators Contest." She paused for a short round of applause. "Wow, that's quite a mouthful," she said.

Everyone laughed.

"And speaking of laughter," said Mrs. Middlemarch. "That will be our topic for tonight's speeches." Then she looked at the six speakers and smiled as wide as she could possibly smile while the audience applauded. Then she returned to the audience. "And it gives me great pride to say that tonight's winner will receive a one thousand dollar college scholarship from our town's newspaper, Awake in Sleepy Hollow."

More applause.

Honey kind of enjoyed the applause, but she knew Clarice was soaking it in like they were clapping only for her. Clarice puffed herself up and waved like she was the Queen of England. Sheesh. Then Honey looked over at six people, three men and three women, sitting off to the side and wearing very stern faces. They were the judges. She recognized four of the people from around town. But two she had never seen before. She swallowed hard. How could she soften their stone faces?

The first speaker was Clarice Kligore. She stood at the podium. Honey could see her knees shaking, but she hung onto the sides of the podium to keep herself steady. Then Honey saw Mayor Kligore standing at the back of the church. He was such a tall man and so imposing that he was hard to miss.

Clarice started her speech. Honey was absolutely correct. Clarice spoke on and on about what a wonderful place Sleepy Hollow was to live. She talked about how funny all the spooky stuff was and how important it is that we laugh at these things because the more you laugh, the more you will learn to appreciate them. That remark made Honey's nerves prickle.

Next up was Noah. He walked to the

podium and just stood there. Mrs. Middlemarch tried to encourage him. But he was frozen. All he could do was stare out at the crowd and the deafening silence that had overtaken the room. He turned toward Mrs. Middlemarch and fainted dead away.

"Oh, dear," cried Mrs. M. "Help, please." She tapped Noah's cheek.

Fortunately, Honey's mom rushed to the rescue and used her nursing skills to revive Noah. She then advised that he be helped off the stage and to "sit this one out."

Everyone applauded anyway.

Finally, after the next two speakers, it was Honey's turn. She stood at the podium and took a deep breath. She looked out at the audience and found her brother, Harry. He was sitting with Honey's turtle backpack next to him. She smiled as a wash of calm rolled over her. "I got you covered, Honey Moon."

Honey nodded and started her speech. She

spoke all about how important it is to laugh. She even spoke about how researchers have studied laughter and how it is contagious. She ended her speech by quoting Ralph Waldo Emerson. "The earth laughs with flowers."

The audience loved her speech. She remained at the podium as the sound of the applause swirled around her. She wanted to cry. But instead, she laughed because doing a great job felt so good. She looked out at her family. It was like their smiles glowed.

Honey received the longest and loudest applause of the evening. With another deep, deep breath Honey returned to her seat. She didn't look, but she could feel Clarice Kligore's glare. It was like spikes headed her way. But she just laughed them off.

"And now," Mrs. Middlemarch said, "our final speaker for tonight will be Darcy Diamond."

The audience applauded as Darcy took her place behind the podium. She did not have gum to spit out this time. Honey thought she looked quite poised. And she was wearing high heels! Well, a small heel anyway. But she never wobbled. Not even once. Honey would have fallen flat on her face—she was certain of that and glad her mom suggested ballet flats.

Darcy started to speak. It was like listening to smooth caramel pouring over the most luscious vanilla ice cream. Honey was dumbstruck. This was, indeed, Darcy Diamond's talent. She hung on to every one of Darcy's words. And so did the audience. Even though she said many of the same things Honey did, Darcy said the things with finesse. Honey was an excellent public speaker, but Darcy was an artist.

Darcy spoke about her favorite, funny movies and talked about why we can laugh at ourselves. She even got the audience to participate in a knock-knock joke.

"Knock, knock," Darcy said.

"Who's there?" called the audience.

"Nobel," Darcy said.

"Nobel who?"

"Nobel. That's why I knocked."

Darcy ended her speech by saying, "People say I talk too much. Well, maybe I do, but I truly hope that my words today might have inspired you to laugh a little more." The audience clapped. And then Darcy said, "The thing is, I know I will just keep getting better and better at public speaking, because after all, I am Darcy Diamond—a diamond in the rough."

199

The audience exploded into applause. They even gave her a standing ovation, and Honey knew that the best girl had won the competition. As Darcy returned to her seat, Honey gave her a big hug. "Congratulations," Honey said.

Darcy took her seat, and that was when Honey noticed Darcy's knees shaking a little bit. Some people get nervous before, some save it for later.

The six speakers sat in their seats as the judges compiled their score sheets and chatted.

"Excellent work, all of you," said Mrs. Middlemarch. "I am so proud!"

"Thank you," Darcy said. "You're a great teacher."

200

"Yeah," the others, even Noah, who never did get to deliver his speech, said. "The best." Finally, the lead judge handed Mrs. Middlemarch a small slip of paper.

Honey grabbed Darcy's hand.

"The winner of the first Sleepy Hollow Young Speakers Contest is Darcy Diamond!"

Darcy jumped out of her seat as the audience applauded and rose to their feet.

Honey stood also. "You are the best talker

in the world!" she shouted over the noise. "And you're my friend."

Darcy turned to Honey. "See," she said. "I knew it was our destiny. Don't you think? I knew we were meant to be friends. And now we are. And by the way, Honey, I thought your speech was just spectacular, but you might try engaging the audience more and—"

"Darcy," Honey said. "Aren't your vocal chords tired by now?"

"I was just thinking," Darcy said, "for when you do the play. Enunciate more, too."

"Okay, okay. Maybe Mrs. Tenure will let you be the dialogue coach."

That was actually a great idea. Honey would speak to Mrs. Tenure about it.

Mrs. Middlemarch returned to the podium. "Juice and cookies are available downstairs in the Fellowship Hall. Please stay and greet our truly talented speakers."

Darcy and Honey headed straight for the cookies. "I am starving," Honey said. "I went without dinner."

"Me, too," Darcy said. "I was so nervous I couldn't eat."

"Really?" Honey asked. "You would never know it."

"Thanks," Darcy said. "And by the way, your new top looks fabulous on you."

"I know," Honey said. "It fits just perfect now."

As Honey munched a chocolate chip cookie, she spied Clarice Kligore with her father. "You said I would win, Daddy. Why didn't I win? Didn't you pay the judges enough?"

Mayor Kligore grabbed Clarice's hand and ushered her out of the room.

Honey laughed. Darcy laughed.

"You know," Honey said. "It is great to laugh."

Darcy took Honey's hand. "Let's go get some more cookies and punch."

And this time Honey didn't mind that Darcy grabbed on to her and didn't let go.

203

Honey Moon's
Top Six Tips for Public Speaking

Try these tips the next time you have to give a report in front of your whole class at school.

1. BE YOURSELF. The audience will know if you're trying too hard. Just be yourself and speak like your speaking to your absolute best friends.

2. DON'T READ YOUR SPEECH. Practice what you're going to say. And if a new thought occurs to you while you're speaking and it's good, go ahead and add it in.

3. TELL GREAT STORIES. Audiences love it when you can tell a great and even funny story that fits your topic. Stories are the best way to make a point.

4. **USE VIDEO** if you can. It's true that sometimes a picture is worth a thousand words.

5. **KNOW WHEN TO STOP TALKING.** Never make your speech last longer than it has to. Don't repeat yourself.

6. **MAKE THEM LAUGH.** Humor is always a great idea. Add a humorous anecdote (a very, very short story that illuminates your subject—it's usually funny) every once in a while. The audience will appreciate it.

206

CREATOR'S NOTES

I am enchanted with the world of Honey Moon, the younger sister of Harry Moon. She is smart and courageous and willing to do anything to help right win out. What a powerhouse.

I wish I had a friend like Honey when I was in school. There is something cool about the way Honey and her friends connect with each other that's very special. When I was Honey's age, I spent most of my time in our family barn taking care of rabbits and didn't hang out with other kids a lot. I think I was always a little bit on the outside.

Maybe that's why I like Honey so much. She lives life with wonderful energy and enthusiasm. She doesn't hesitate to speak her mind. And she demands that adults pay attention to her because more often than not, the girl knows what she is talking about. And she often finds herself getting into all kinds of crazy adventures.

We all need real friends like Honey. Growing up is quite an adventure and living it with girlfriends that you love builds friendships that can last a lifetime. That's the point, I think, of Honey's enchanted world—life is just better when you work it out with friends.

I am happy that you have decided to join me, along with author Suzanne Brooks Kuhn, in the enchanted world of Honey Moon. I would love for you to let us know about any fun ideas you have for Honey in her future stories. Visit harrymoon.com and let us know.

See you again in our next visit to the enchanted world of Honey Moon!

MARK ANDREW POE

The Enchanted World of Honey Moon creator Mark Andrew Poe never thought about creating a town where kids battled right and wrong. His dream was to love and care for animals, specifically his friends in the rabbit community.

Along the way, Mark became successful in all sorts of interesting careers. He entered the print and publishing world as a young man and his company did really, really well. Mark also became a popular and nationally sought-after health care advocate for the care and well-being of rabbits.

Years ago, Mark came up with the idea of a story about a young boy with a special connection to a world of magic, all revealed through a remarkable rabbit friend. Mark worked on his idea for several years before building a collaborative creative team to help him bring his idea to life.

Harry Moon was born. The team was thrilled when Mark introduced Harry's enchanting sister, Honey Moon. Boy, did she pack an unexpected punch!

In 2014, Mark began a multi-book project to launch *The Amazing Adventures of Harry Moon* and *The Enchanted World of Honey Moon* into the youth marketplace. Harry and Honey are kids who understand the difference between right and wrong. Kids who tangle with magic and forces unseen in a town where "every day is Halloween night." Today, Mark and the creative team continue to work on the many stories of Harry and Honey and the characters of Sleepy Hollow. He lives in suburban Chicago with his wife and his 25 rabbits.

SUZANNE BROOKS KUHN

Suzanne Brooks Kuhn is a mom and author with a passion for children's stories. Suzanne brings her precocious childhood experiences and sassy storytelling ability to her creative team in weaving the magical stories found in *The Enchanted World of Honey Moon*. Suzanne lives with her husband in an 1800's farmhouse nestled in the countryside of central Virginia.

BE SURE TO READ THE
CONTINUING AND ENCHANTED
ADVENTURES OF HONEY MOON.